A Time to Change

Country Stories and Local History from John Lea

I need to acknowledge the help given by several people particularly Richard Thorneycroft, John and Sheila Bowler, Norman Buxton, Graham Hefford and the late Jack Trueman. But there are many more who have confirmed a story or added a little more detail to one. To them all, I say a big thank you.

Photographs by Celia R. Lea

The drawing of a trout on page 76 is by courtesy of the artist, G. Ashley Hunter, whose wonderful illustrations feature so much in my previous three books

Three bestselling books from John Lea available from Churnet Valley:

Down the Cobbled Stones
My Countryside
The Peover Eye

CHURNET VALLEY BOOKS
1 King Street, Leek, Staffordshire. ST13 5NW 01538 399033
© John Lea and Churnet Valley Books 2004
ISBN 1 904546 18 8

CONTENTS

Some dialect words used in this book:

owt = anything

yer = you or yours

mun = must

mayn't = may not

canna = can not

slatter = to lose

fashin = to top and tail vegetables

A Time to Change: Old Gabriel

The young land agent was too officious for Gabriel's liking and he particularly resented him striding into the churchyard and giving him orders.

"I work for th' vicar not yer estate."

"Perhaps you should remember who the vicar owes his living to. Anyway her ladyship would like to see her parents grave tidied up."

"Arr, it's a request from her ladyship is it? Then that's different."

The Squire's wife was one of the few gentry that Gabriel held in respect and not just because she always remembered him at Christmas. As for the estate's land agent, Gabriel rudely turned his back on him and began to scythe.

It wasn't long before he was interrupted again, this time by his daughter's scolding voice coming from behind him. "Dad you've never changed the time of the church clock, it is still not right."

"I've always set th' clock by that there church sundial an' am not going to change now," he told her crossly.

"But Dad," rebuke and frustration rang through Hannah's answer. "The trains must run to London time. When people hear the church clock strike they think that they can easily catch the train, then when they get to the station it's gone because your clock's slow."

"Slow! Slow! It's not slow, that' there is th' sun (stabbing his pipe towards the watery afternoon sky). Maybe you young 'uns think that yer can change th' world but yer canna' change th' sun."

Seeing Hannah's irritation he added, "if them clever beggars want th' train to go at 8 o'clock why do they call it th' 8.15?"

Gabriel picked up his scythe, turned his back on his daughter and began to swing it between the gravestones with a rhythmical, almost lazy, action that could be sustained all day.

Hannah was furious with him. She had always been conscious that her dad was old, even at school other girls had thought he was her granddad. Now, working for the railway and mixing with the incomers, she realised that he was not just old but obstinate as well.

With the railway other changes had come to the village. Not only had it brought work into the village for some, others it enabled to travel or even take jobs outside their isolated farming community, and without being jogged to death on a shaky old trap behind a stupid, smelly pony.

The 8.15 morning train was now called the milk train because many of the local dairy farmers used it to send their milk into Manchester - before the railway came the only outlet for that milk had been to make it into cheese or butter on the farm and sell those products at local markets. There was one problem though; it meant getting up earlier to milk the cows if the milk was to get to the station in time for the milk train. That was when one or two farmers used the church clock as an excuse for being late.

The biggest change to Hannah's life though was not so much her job at the station but the assistant stationmaster George. 'George is so sophisticated and experienced.' But then being brought up in Knutsford had given him lots of opportunities to go to the theatre and things. 'Oh I do fancy him' she mused but just when he got chatting to her that morning two angry farmers came in asking, "where's the train?"

"Its gone on time," said George.

"On time; on time; the church clock's only just struck eight!" Pulling out his big pocket watch George said, "This is the time! Not that church clock set by some old fool's sundial."

Then returning his watch and tapping his pocket, he added, "Our trains run by London time."

Well there had been a right barney, Hannah had crept away thinking that George would never talk to her again if he found out that the old fool was her dad.

Then George finally did it. He asked her if she would walk out with him on Sunday afternoon. Hannah was so excited that she persuaded her mother to help her use the hot tongs to crimp a tight wave in her lovely brown hair.

She led him down the lane away from the village and towards the style down by the brook where, Hannah hoped, they would not meet any of the village children. She knew that if they realized she was keen on George they would tease her unmercifully and probably shout 'puff puff' every time they saw her.

She hardly spoke a word to George as they wandered along because he was so knowledgeable, telling her all about Knutsford - he had even been on the train as far as Manchester. She had never been there and he was just offering to take her when who should climb over the style in front but her dad.

Old Gabriel stopped, leaned against the fence to light his pipe and between puffs asked, "Who's this then?"

When she shyly told him, Old Gabriel took a few more puffs then said, "You mean him as wants to change th' time of th' sun?"

When Hannah's blushes confirmed it, George, officiously pulled out his pocket watch and tried to explain the difference between a sundial and London time. But Gabriel turned his back to shelter his pipe while he struck another match. After a few puffs he turned back and, stabbing towards the lad with his pipe stem, said, "Well I'll tell thee lad - that there sun 'as bin keeping time through th'ages; now if yer tries to make life go faster than it's meant to then yer'll soon be in a plot next to my old sundial."

With that he stuck his pipe back in his mouth, took a deep puff or two and set off on his way. Suddenly he stopped and turned back to call out. "Eh lad - Missus'll have tea on at tea time, so if yer knows when that is, maybe yer'll join us, eh?"

Hannah wasn't Gabriel's only child. 16 years before she was born, his Missus (he never called her anything else) had given birth to Jimmy. They had hoped for a larger family but sadly, after Jimmy, two babies were lost in infancy and a third through a very difficult childbirth, which left his wife very debilitated. At that time they were living in a tied cottage belonging to the farm where Gabriel worked. The long hours on the farm and nursing his seriously ill wife changed Gabriel into a prematurely old man.

The vicar came to his rescue by offering him the Sexton's job and with it the tenancy of a small cottage on the outskirts of the village. With the reduced workload and flexible hours both his own health and that of his wife's slowly recovered.

By that time Jimmy had already left school and was working on the farm with his father. When the family moved house he carried on with his job, he just had a longer walk to his work. When a few years had gone by he met Beth, who was a live-in maid at the big house, and after a suitable courtship they wanted to get married. Jimmy's boss offered him the same tied cottage that had formerly been Gabriel's.

The Sexton's job was not full-time, which allowed Gabriel to do some part-time gardening around the village and to spend quite a bit of time in his own garden. Had it been a little larger, he often thought, he would have kept a cow to produce his own milk, but as it was he could grow all the vegetables they could use themselves plus quite a surplus to sell. And there was his small orchard. He was extremely proud of the quality of his fruit, five varieties of apple, the best of which could be stored down his cellar until the following summer and on one splendid pear tree an ancient craftsman had grafted four different varieties, ranging from a juicy variety that ripened in early August to one that needed a frost in November to make it anything like edible and only then when it had been stored down the cellar until spring. Two plum trees and half a dozen damsons growing in the boundary hedge completed a very healthy little orchard.

In the autumn Gabriel took his abundant harvest. Just as the four varieties of pears came over a period of four months, there were also blackberries ripening in the hedgerows to pick in August and September, plums ripening late in August and damsons in early September, followed by the early apples and pears making it a busy month. And when Gabriel took his harvest he did just that, he took it into the back kitchen and said, "Here yer are Missus, here's another eight pounds of damsons for yer."

That his Missus had to sort, stew and bottle them on through the evening got from Gabriel no more than an appreciative glance at the results. He just took it for granted that his role was to grow and pick and hers was to cook, bottle and store, and to be fair both were content with their lot. For them married life was a working partnership which, if both put in their fair share of effort, fulfiled the basic needs of life.

Neither had known any other life, she had been an orphan who had 'lived in' working as a maid on the farm where Gabriel worked, and he was well past his youth when he decided that she would do. After all from when she was a skinny 12-year-old he had watched her at work both in the house and when she helped out on the farm at busy times. Many were the times she brought the baggin to him when he was working down the fields and in the autumn he carried baskets of fruit from the farm orchard into the farmhouse back kitchen and said, "Here you are, here's another ten pounds of apples for yer."

When he announced in the pub that they were getting married he said, "Her mayn't be beautiful but her'll be useful." Hadn't he watched her enough years to know just how useful she would be. So after they were married, when he brought in his ten pounds of apples, he just had to add 'Missus' to his "here's another ten pounds for yer".

Working with nature gave Gabriel the opportunity to study it. Although when he was a lad he used to laugh at old men chasing after butterflies with a net, now he could happily sit for a half hour just watching the many different species visiting the flowers in his cottage garden, which of course his Missus looked after. He did sometimes curse the hundreds of the large white butterfly's caterpillars that hatched out on his cabbage plants but his dozen hens enjoyed the feast when he picked them off and threw them into the hen pen.

His interest in nature had developed at an early age when he and Tom, his younger brother, rambled the lanes and fields. When Tom asked what this or that was he tried to answer and what he didn't know he asked from his parents. As they could barely read or write they usually couldn't answer either. The solution came when his Sunday school teacher, deciding to give him a prize for good attendance, asked his parents what sort of book he would like. Gabriel got his nature book and he could now answer his own and young Tom's questions.

At the age of 11 he left school and started full-time work on the farm, and of course at the same time he also considered himself too old for Sunday school. They gave him a Bible as a parting present, but it was the book on nature he turned to time and time again.

Although those early days on the farm were long they were not too arduous. He spent many long hours scaring birds off newly sown crops or ripening grain. To some it would have been boring but to Gabriel each day was filled with interest. More than once he saw the lightning speed of a stoat as it caught a rabbit and many times he stood motionless as a hunting fox passed close by, and of course there were bird's nests in the hedgerows and butterflies flitting from wildflower to wildflower.

When he wasn't in school Tom joined him and later took his wildlife interest more seriously and became a trainee gamekeeper. And now he was the head keeper for the estate. Having to talk to his boss at the big house and mix with the guests on shooting days had made Tom talk more correctly than Gabriel, and with his tweed suit and more youthful looks, strangers would never think that they were brothers.

Not being a large estate, Tom only had a youth as trainee gamekeeper to help him, so he often called on Gabriel to give him a hand perhaps at busy times or when there was a chance that poachers were about.

It wasn't poachers worrying Gabriel this windy October day, it was his two grandsons, Rob and Jack. Jimmy's twin lads were nearing school leaving age. He had heard how they had been getting into mischief but had put it down to just childish fun. That was until this morning. Of all the stupid things to do they came pinching apples out of the vicarage garden - and when he was working there.

What made it worse they were on the way to his house. When there was a do on at the big house, their mum, Beth, would have to work on Saturday and with Jimmy working on the farm the two lads came to spend the day with him and their grandma.

The vicar caught them under the apple tree and brought them to Gabriel. "These are your grandson's and they were up in my best keeping apple; what are you going to do about them?"

"I'll have a talk to their Dad, it's better he deals with them himself." With that he sent them on their way to his Missus and after finishing his work he walked up to Jimmy's cottage to have a talk to him in his dinner hour.

"I blame schooling," old Gabriel said. "When I wer' their age I would have been too tired from hard work to get into mischief." He pulled on his pipe in reflective thought. "What do they expect keeping lads in school until they're 13. They need some hard graft, by heck, arr, that 'ud keep 'em out of trouble."

"But Dad I want these lads to have a better chance than I had. Now with the train running through and with a better education maybe they'll get a job in town. Something where they're not outside in all weathers or down on their knees weeding between turnips."

"Well maybe lad, but what sort of a job needs you to be in school until you're thirteen, eh?"

Jimmy couldn't argue with his father nowadays. When he was younger he could. They used to have lively discussions but in recent years as old Gabriel's back got more bowed he had become more cantankerous. As Jimmy was having a rare two hours off between dinner and Saturday afternoon milking he decided to walk down to the village and deal with the two lads himself. Gabriel left him to it and, with a chunk of Jimmy's bread and cheese, headed towards the pub.

Jimmy pondered as he walked along as to what he would tell his boys. He had stolen apples himself and from that very same tree - but he hadn't been caught. Okay, yes, the vicar had shaken his fist at him and shouted, "I know it was you!" But he hadn't caught him so he couldn't really have been sure. Though in fairness to the lads the old vicar had retired and there was a younger one now with a quicker turn of speed.

So, Jimmy pondered, should he clip their ears for stealing, or should he clip their ears for getting caught? In the end he decided just to clip their ears and let them work it out for themselves.

Although there wasn't a crossroads in the village, four lanes left it in different directions. Gabriel's cottage was just outside the village, the church and vicarage were in the centre and the pub lay at the end of the village on the lane that led to Jimmy's cottage. There was a convenient and much used footpath across the fields between the pub and Gabriel's cottage. It was dark when he came out of the pub and set off across this footpath, and he had crossed one field when he first heard it. "It was an owl, of course it was an owl", Gabriel muttered to himself as he tramped quickly homeward, "But then again, was it too drawn out for an owl?"

The October gale that had swept the autumn leaves into deep drifts behind the field hedge had long subsided to just a gusty breeze. As the old man reached for the stile those now dry leaves rustling and crackling under his unsteady feet made the owl's hoot sound a little weirder still. Pausing to burp loudly he was conscious that he shouldn't have stayed in the pub all afternoon - that last pint had been one too many on an empty stomach.

Although his head and shoulders were above the top step, to Old Gabriel's fuddled mind it was a mountain, and deciding that hands and knees might be more prudent than a moving stile he slid down and wandered unsteadily along the hedge to look for a gap. The long plaintive wailing hoot made the hairs prickle on his neck and that was when he saw it - out there in the field, white and formless floating towards him. Although clouds now hid the moon there was enough light to make the thing glow. He stopped, rooted by fear, as it too seemed to stop and take a deep breath, then let out another haunting hoot. The old man moaned in fright and rushed back towards the stile; when he glanced over his shoulder the thing seemed to be following him When there came another eerie hoot from behind him he took the stile in his stride. Well not quite because there was an awful tearing sound at the top but he didn't let it stop him. Landing on his feet, and shaky though they were, his old legs propelled him quickly homeward.

The two lads chuckled quietly as they climbed out of the ditch. "I didn't know Grandpa could run like that," said one.

"Nor did I. Wasn't it good that owl hooting back just at the right moment?"

"Great. It gets our own back for him telling Dad about the apples and us getting a clip round the ear. I suppose we'd better go and get Grandma's sheet off that scarecrow. She told us to get him home for tea and the way he was going across that field he should be there soon."

"She promised us a treat if he was home in time; what it will be?"

There had to be a good reason for Gabriel to take too much drink and this time it was his brother Tom. He had come to him in the pub and said, "I had a tip off that some poachers will be out tonight, how about giving me a hand?"

"I'm getting too old for it, chasing round fields after young fellas is no good for me. "Yer mun get someone else."

"There is no one else. I'll take the lad with me but I've heard it's long nets behind Strawberry Wood. Anyway I'm not that much younger than you so I don't want to catch them. I find its easier to let them get set up and then slip out of the wood behind them and just cut the lines in their nets. Not only will they not catch any rabbits they'll not use the nets again until they've repaired them. I need you to watch for them at one end, while we watch the other."

"Oh, all right then but I'm not getting mixed up in owt, if I see 'em I'll just walk across and tell yer, and I'm off."

So that was how he came to sink a few more beers than he intended; he needed the dutch courage. And with only that bit of cheese and bread he had from Jimmy's, they were on an empty stomach.

The ghost fright on the footpath and the run home sobered him considerably, and a cup of tea and some good food pretty well completed the task. He knew he had made a fool of himself but there had been no one there to see him, had there? The way those two lads were grinning over their tea they knew something - 'an come to think of it ,if that wer' no owl, it wern't a ghost either'.

"All right lads I think I know." Gabriel said smiling back at them.

When tea was over the lads helped their Grandma with the washing-up while Gabriel got his things ready for the night's activities. One stout blackthorn knob stick, one warm topcoat and his old tweed hat - and he was ready to go.

"I promised yer Dad I'd walk home with yer in case yer got frightened in the dark; yer never know what yer might hear out there - and anyway we don't want yer in any more mischief do we, eh?"

So the three of them walked companionably along the lane and through the village. Passing the pub on the other side of the village Gabriel thought of the ghostly owl and was glad they had come round by the lane this time. They walked to within 100 yards of Jimmy's cottage where Gabriel left them and walked back to his poacher watching post for evening. It was a cold but pleasant night, most of the time the clouds hid the half-moon but occasionally it peeped between them lighting up the hedgerows. He took up a spot well back from a gateway where he was hidden in the shadows by bushes.

A couple of hours went by without incident. When the moon started to peep between the clouds for longer periods he became sure that there would be no long-netting that night; it needed a dark windy night. With the moon out and just a bit of breeze it was far from ideal.

Gabriel kept his position for a bit longer and then decided he'd had enough. As he walked towards the gate a man stepped through it with a gun in his hand just as the moon broke through again. They faced each other frozen in startled fear. Grief, thought Gabriel, this isn't what I am here for, he isn't after rabbits with a long-net. "Evenin'," Gabriel said as pleasantly as he could. "I wer' just taking the dog for a walk an' he ran off in here, I've bin whistling for him but he won't come "

He gave a demonstration whistle for his imaginary dog but with the gaps in his teeth and a sudden complete lack of spittle in his mouth the sound that came out would not have been heard 10 yards away. The man just stood looking at him with the gun held ready across his stomach. Gabriel kept his eyes on the gate as he walked towards it. "I hope I haven't disturbed whatever it is yer after," he said. "Anyway me old dog's probably gone home by now. Enjoy yer night's shooting."

The man turned watchfully as Gabriel stepped past him through the gate. Fortunately he was at the pub end of the village and it was only a matter of minutes before he was leaning on the bar with a shaky pint in his hand. He was marvelling at his quick thinking considering how scared he'd been earlier that evening, "Mind yer, I wer' scared enough," he said, and looked round guiltily in case someone was listening.

It wasn't long before Tom joined him. "I gave up," Tom said, "it's too light, they won't be out tonight."

"Which way did yer come?" Gabriel asked.

"I came across the field to where you were supposed to be waiting. A dark cloud just hid everything but I could hear you walking out ahead of me. Why didn't you stop? When I shouted you seemed to go faster -you were in a rush to get a pint."

"Arr I wer' but that wern't me in front of yer - that wer' a man with a gun."

Tom wanted to know what the man with a gun looked like but Gabriel would only say "it wer' too dark."

"But you said the moon came out, so you must have seen his face?"

"Arr, he wer' a tough looking character but I didn't rightly look at him."

"Come on man you must have looked at him, the moon was shining right on him?"

"I wer' just looking at the gate. Eh, remember this." Gabriel tugged at where a pellet had scarred his right ear. "I got this chasing a man with a gun for yer once before and I've still got a pellet in me shoulder. No! If there're guns, I'm off home."

After taking a long drink at his beer, Tom said. "Anyway he was a stranger - and a stranger with a gun is bad news for a keeper. I've heard that some are using the trains, coming out of town on the last one at night and then going back on the first next morning. Anyway on a moonlit night and with a gun he would be after my roosting pheasants."

Gabriel said. "Well then you mun get that village constable out because I'm having nothing to do with it."

Gabriel had a busy week coming up, it was the church harvest festival the following Sunday and it was usually one of the proudest days in his year. There was no flower or vegetable show in the village so the only time that the gardeners had a chance to compare their produce was at the harvest festival. Each brought their best and for Gabriel it meant that he spent most of the week choosing the five best carrots, his best cauliflower or cabbage and of course the pick of his fruit.

He even got involved with his Missus bottling pears. Mind you, not to help but to make sure that at least two bottles had the biggest and best shaped pears showing round the outside of the glass. It was the best of these that would go to the harvest festival. He had learned the hard way not to rely on one bottle because one year, despite the skill of his Missus, his chosen bottle's rubber washer had failed to seal as the contents had cooled. No seal, no vacuum and the fruit wouldn't keep. No matter how good the pears looked his Missus wasn't going to let him take what would have been a failure to the church.

There was one vegetable that he didn't grow and it was turnips; he had enough of working in them when he was a farm worker. It had been nothing but a backbreaking crop. Weeding among them in the summer and pulling and fashing off the roots and tops, when they were covered with frost in the autumn, had put him off growing turnips. As for potatoes - one of the farmers, with acres to select from, nearly always managed to get a better potato, but Gabriel took some beating on most other vegetables. Not that there was any prizes or official competition but after morning service those old farmers and gardeners would potter around the front of the church comparing and discussing the pride of their season's work.

Of course Gabriel wouldn't say anything boastful but his bent old shoulders would straighten a little with pride. The last vicar who had entered into the spirit of the game sometimes included a special prayer in the service thanking God for looking after Gabriel's carrots or his cauliflowers or whatever was exceptional that year. It wasn't just vegetables either, just to show how clever they were the baker made a large loaf in the shape of a sheaf of wheat, the dressmaker embroidered a pair of napkins and the grocer made sure that there were also a few delicious items with his name on.

The new vicar thought that none of this was in the true spirit of a harvest festival and preached a sermon to the effect that the harvest festival was not a time to boast how clever you were but rather a time to say a humble thank you to the Creator. One year later, when it became obvious that some of his words had, like the parable of the sower, fallen on stony ground, he decided to sow a different seed and suggested a village flower and vegetable show.

Of course every activity within the village had to have the permission of the squire from the big house; the surrounding farmers and most of the villagers were his tenants. Village democracy was only allowed to work if he agreed with the decision. Even in church the squire and his wife sat in a little pew box on one side of the church, some six-foot above the other pews. It was known by the villagers as "the halfway to heaven pew" but Gabriel had been heard to mutter, "When the good Lord measures down from above it might be that it's halfway to hell."

Trying to convert the villagers from judging their vegetables at the harvest festival, the new vicar tackled Gabriel one day when he was working in the churchyard. "This habit of judging your vegetables in church is sinful you know, Gabriel. You seem to forget that the good Lord made them all."

"Arr maybe but it's hard work that makes some better than others. Yet Vicar, yer happy that people judge who's best in church."

"No one is better than anyone else before God."

"Then why does th' squire sit six foot above everyone else, eh?"

As the squire had the final say in his appointment the vicar suddenly remembered he had a parishioner to visit and went hurriedly on his way. Anyway with the squire's blessing a committee was formed and plans were made to hold the first flower and vegetable show the following year, which meant that this was the last of the traditional harvests and Gabriel wanted to make the most of it.

The trunk of his four variety pear towered so far above his other fruit trees that for a year or two his Missus insisted it was too dangerous for him to climb a ladder up there. Hannah had climbed the ladder instead, and picked them for him before, but it was no good asking her this year because she was mooning about George so much that when she helped her mother to sort some of the fruit she missed some damaged ones.

In the sequence of ripening, the third pear variety was the best looking, but they were still on the tree, so with the promise of goodies for their tea the two grandsons came one evening after school to help him out. At first one held the ladder while the other climbed up to the dizzy heights but it wasn't long before he started to shake it instead of steadying it. Gabriel sorted them out and decided to hold the ladder himself. When a well aimed pear 'accidentally' landed on his head he realized that perhaps the two lads were getting a bit out of hand nowadays.

The fruit was stored on wooden trays in the cellar but first it had to be carefully inspected because any bit of rot or damage could turn the whole tray rotten. This was one time when Gabriel sorted the fruit himself, not that he wanted to interfere with his Missus's work but as well as the bottle pears he wanted to select the best half dozen to place on a plate at the church harvest.

It wasn't just getting the produce ready that kept Gabriel busy; the vicar also wanted the churchyard to be tidy for the harvest festival. Gabriel was never keen to mow between all the graves, not just because it would take a long time but mainly because of the barn owls. The long grass in the churchyard was the hunting ground for a pair who nested each year in a nearby farm building. When the new vicar came he criticised Gabriel for the untidy grass in the old part of the graveyard but after Gabriel had persuaded him to sit with him one evening and watch the hunting owls it was agreed that he should just mow the paths through the new grave area - in case of sudden need. For the harvest though he was to mow a wider strip along the main path and round the church doors, and of course sweep all the paths clean.

It was the tradition to distribute the harvest gifts amongst the poor in and around the village - and there were some poor. Their welfare was in the hands of the vestry committee who met monthly under the chairmanship of the vicar to decide to whom the gifts would go. It was not just the harvest gifts they controlled, there was also a charity fund that enabled them to buy and distribute coal in the winter months and secondhand clothing, particularly where there was a widow with small children.

Gabriel would have nothing to do with them, in years gone by he'd been too close to needing their help. Several times in the winter months when there were few gardening jobs to supplement his small wage they had lived on a very meagre fare, but his home-grown vegetables and fruit store had helped him and his Missus scrape through. In recent years with Hannah working full-time their finances were much eased.

The vestry committee's work was done very discreetly; the members distributed the gifts themselves and never talked outside the committee, but of course everyone in the village knew who was being helped and why. Gabriel was not averse to dishing out some of his own surplus with equal discretion but if it was to a widow he was careful to go in daylight and not to stop many minutes. He had learned the hard way of village gossip. When first he and his Missus moved into the village, of course she was not well so Gabriel carried the house water from the village pump each morning. It was a new experience for him, after living in a lonely farm cottage, mixing with so many villagers each day, and he had always been a chatty sort of character. One particular widow, who seemed to be at the pump at the same time as Gabriel most mornings, was very sympathetic about his wife's illness and before long began to call at their home to see if she could help. With his wife in bed for most of the day Gabriel was appreciative, that was until Tom took him on one side and said, "There's a rumour going round the village that you're keeping two women." It had made him very aware of the dangers of gossip in a close village society.

He earned a little extra money helping Tom on shooting days but he didn't really enjoy it. The gentry seemed to treat him as some sort of old duffer whereas they treated Tom with respect, and yet he had taught Tom much of what he knew. He stayed away from them as much as he could and hated it when he had to doff his hat to the toffs.

One thing that pleased him was George; he liked the lad and particularly because not only had he started to attend church with Hannah, but he also seemed to get on with both the gentry and the ordinary villagers equally. The difference between the church clock and the station clock was never mentioned again - the trains ran on London time and the church services were held on local time. Many of the parishioners relied on a sundial themselves and those who had watches or clocks just shrugged their shoulders and set them to whichever time suited them.

The autumn turned into a really nasty one, not only was there a lot of rain, by mid November there was a heavy frost followed by a fall of snow. Worried about his late pears still clinging on to the tree, although one or two frosts helped to ripen and sweeten them, Gabriel was determined to have them in the cellar in case of a really keen frost. Rob and Jack came to his rescue again on the Saturday morning. They picked the pears without too much fooling about this time, although Gabriel kept clear of the ladder.

A spell of warm weather in early December brought both his late cauliflowers and his winter cabbages to head all at once. Although he gave one or two slightly damaged ones to needy widows - in daylight of course, he and his Missus decided to have a day at the market, to sell the surplus including some fruit and to do some Christmas shopping. The market town was a good five miles away and as it was raining; Gabriel had persuaded a neighbouring farmer, Jim Slater, to let him put his two heavy sacks of greens and the smaller ones of fruit on to Jim's farm cart, which was already loaded with potatoes. The cart was already carrying enough for the one horse so there was no chance of a ride for themselves.

Several villagers made the journey including the village joiner and his wife who were carrying chairs that he had made that autumn. He carried three and his wife carried two and they had tied them over their shoulders in such a way that they acted as umbrellas. For the rest of them it was a matter of trudging along inside overcoats that got heavier as they soaked up more rain.

Gabriel and his Missus sold their produce fairly quickly, as did the joiner, and with their shopping also done, the four of them, their heavy and wet overcoats weighing on their shoulders, set out to walk back together. But when Jim Slater caught up with them with his empty cart they readily accepted his offer of a lift. They were soon all chatting happily together and when they came to a pub along the roadside the farmer decided his horse needed a rest.

The two women seldom went inside a public house so it was quite a treat for them to sit chatting over a beer. The conversation covered a variety of subjects including the farmer asking, "I'm surprised

Gabriel that you've never had a dog?" "Well I thought of it but I couldn't take one into other people's gardens, and then he could also be a bit of a nuisance round the church."

His Missus said. "He used to work a dog at the farm and he was always shouting and swearing at it, so much so that it ran around in circles in confusion. When he asked me to marry him I said that I could put up with him but not if he had a dog."

"So you can see why I never had a dog."

The joiner joined in now. "There's four men on the table behind you and one of 'em's taking a lot of interest in you Gabriel."

Gabriel looked over his shoulder straight into the cold hard eyes of the man he had met in that moonlit gateway.

"So you've never had a dog then?"

"No! And I'll bet that you've never had a gun either?"

Turning back to his companions Gabriel said, "let's drink up, it'll soon be night and funny things seemed to happen to me in the dark."

It was in Jim Slater's farm buildings where the barn owls nested. He and Gabriel had been friends for many years. Gabriel didn't seek out farm work but when Jim was stuck for help he often responded. When they had all climbed up onto the cart Jim said, "I've been meaning to ask you; we're thrashing a stack of oats next week and I could do with another man, how about it?"

It would be a little extra money and Jim's Missus always dished up some good food - and she made the best beer in the village. So Gabriel said, "Arr I reckon I'll be there."

The portable thrashing machine was a fairly new invention; it had replaced the old thrashing barn in which men had toiled away through the winter months. With no means of self-propulsion it had to be hauled from farm to farm by a team of horses. Even the steam engine that powered it was just a stationery one mounted on a sturdy wooden frame with strong cart wheels, and it too had to be hauled about behind another horse team. All this took a considerable amount of time and effort particularly to get it set up level and with the thresher in line with the steam engine.

Expecting just to be working on the stack, which would keep him out of most of the dust and smoke, Gabriel was not pleased to find that the thrashing contractor had yet to set the machine up and that he had to start the day pushing and pulling and heaving to get the thrashing box set up square and level.

It was mid-morning baggin time before they had everything lined up so they took it before starting to thrash. After a glass of weak but tasty beer and a thick cheese butty, Gabriel climbed up a ladder to the top of the stack and began to toss the oat sheaves down on to the thrashing box. It was steady rhythmic work placing each sheaf the right way round for the man on the box to cut the band and feed them evenly into the drum. Once he had got a start in the stack Jim came on to pass the sheaves to Gabriel who in turn pitched them onto the box. There was no break in the work until dinner, when they were glad of the hour to eat and relax.

They worked all through the afternoon with just one pause when Mrs Slater came round to give another glass of homebrewed beer to each worker in turn - and it was good. Tea was replacing it on most farms but because it was expensive the can of tea that came out to the farmworkers was usually too weak to be tasty. Gabriel added, "Arr, yer canna beat a glass of your beer, Missus."

When it became too dark to work, and it was time for afternoon baggin, they just wiped the dust off their face and hands before tucking into Mrs Slater's cheese and jam butties, washed down this time with a fairly potent brew of tea. Afterwards Jim and his men went to do the milking while Gabriel wandered homeward.

The next morning the stack got lower and of course the thrashing box remained the same height so pitching the sheaves up and on to it became harder. The two men exchanged jobs about every half hour, even so Gabriel was glad when dinner time came and he could go and sample Mrs Slater's potato ash followed by plum dumpling. After too short a rest they picked up their pitchforks and started again. When they were nearing the bottom of the stack Tom came to give his two fox terriers some action. "Ratting is the best exercise for these dogs, they are a lot keener after a fox if they've killed a few rats," Tom said.

The stack had been built on a layer of timber topped with loose straw and the rats stayed under it until the very end. There was only nine rats and the terriers killed with such a quick bite that neither got bitten, nor did any get away. Jim said. "In the New Year when we thrash that stack of wheat there'll be a lot more than nine rats."

Standing companionably side-by-side leaning on their pitchforks, when the straw moved just in front of them the two old men, both well past their nimble years, instinctively stamped on what they presumed was a hidden rat. Unfortunately Gabriel was a fraction quicker and Jim's hobnailed boot came down firmly on top of his. The fact that Mrs Slater was walking across the farmyard with afternoon baggin stopped him from saying what he might have as he hopped around on one leg. The rest of the thrashing crew teased him all through baggin until he got up in disgust and set off to limp home.

He had barely got out of the farmyard gate when the vicar hailed him cheerily. "Gabriel, just the man I want to see, I need a grave digging. Why are you limping?"

He'd never known the old spinster, she had left the village about 70 years before but her dying wish was to be buried in her parent's grave so he was digging in the old part of the graveyard. He had to do a bit with a scythe around the area first. He and the vicar found it difficult to pinpoint the grave from the old church records but they knew from past experience that they were not very accurate in this part of the churchyard. Gabriel discovered that his rat stamping foot was also the one he used on the spade. It really hurt. It would take him two days to dig it so there was no time to change his mind - once he had started to dig she was going in this hole, right or wrong. With two coffins already in the grave he wouldn't have to go down the full depth, so he planned to dig to about 3 foot on the first day and finish it on the second.

Disgruntled with his sore foot he sat down on the lip of the grave to light his pipe - that was when he saw the dog. It was a nuisance of a mongrel but his grandson's assured him it was a good ratter. Never kept under control by its owner, the dog had started to follow the two boys around on the Saturdays when they were at his house. Between them they had even caught a couple of rats from under his hen house, and now it was scratching after mice by one of the gravestones. A well-aimed stone sent it scuttling towards its home, and Gabriel decided to do the same.

After tea he would have liked to go for a consoling pint but his foot ached too much so he sat miserably in front of the fire. His Missus filled a bowl with hot water and put some salt in. "Put your smelly old foot in that". she said. It did seem to soothe the pain away and surprisingly the next morning it was much better. It hardly hurt at all as he sunk the spade in with his usual rhythm. It was a pleasant morning and this was a job that he enjoyed because he liked to be on his own in the peace of the graveyard. Taking a break to have a puff at his pipe he watched contentedly as a flock of crows flew overhead and some blackbirds argued with a song thrush over the ripening berries on a holly bush.

That was when the grave side fell in. It wasn't a big fall but it was obvious that he had been digging too close to the next grave, and a small area of it gave way. When he sunk his spade into the loose fall of soil it struck something and routing it out he found he had an arm. Not the whole arm but just from the elbow down with the hand complete. This sort of thing had happened before, so Gabriel quickly covered it in the loose soil on the bank of the grave before any nosy villagers could see it, his intention being to bury it later in the bottom of the grave he was digging.

"Arr, yer a great cook Missus." Gabriel said as he tucked into his homegrown potatoes and cabbage along with the rabbit he had snared behind his garden. It was a very contented old man who wandered back to the grave after dinner - that was until he discovered the arm had gone. From the scratch marks in the soil it would seem that the stupid mongrel had dug it up.

When he had searched the graveyard without success he headed towards the dog's home with a certain amount of apprehension. The dog wasn't owned by one of the old villagers; since the railway had come the squire had raised a bit of money by selling one or two cottages to outsiders who commuted to work by train. This was one such family; and with her husband off for the day the wife just let the dog out. She had been warned that the local farmers wouldn't tolerate a wandering dog but she resented the advice.

Gabriel knocked on the door. "I come to see if yer dog's come home Missus."

"What my dog does has nothing to do with you."

"I wondered if he might have brought something back with him?"

"He hasn't been anywhere, he's been here with me all morning. Now if you don't mind I have better things to do than talk."

As the door close in his face, Gabriel muttered, "Arr well if it's chewing on an arm in front of yer fire yer'd have something to say to me then, eh?"

He liked to finish digging a grave on the day before a funeral even though this one wasn't until two o'clock, which was a nuisance itself because he wouldn't have time to fill the grave before dark and, being Friday, it meant that he would have to work again on the Saturday morning.

The funeral went well; apparently the old lady had been housekeeper to a wealthy industrialist who had died and left her comfortably off. Some of her great nieces and nephews looked equally comfortably off to Gabriel's eye as he watched discreetly. Not too discreetly though - he had learnt that when there were wealthy mourners round the grave it paid to be seen with his spade in his hand. It worked this time too because one of the smartly dressed ladies came over to him and handing him two guineas she said, "Thank you for digging the grave, my good man. As none of us live close by, will you kindly take care of the grave for us?"

Gabriel smiled, nodded his head, and even doffed his hat.

As expected he had to go back on Saturday morning to finish filling in and tidying up about the grave, then he did some work in the vicarage garden before wandering back home for dinner.

"Where are those two lads, Missus?"

"They have gone off with that mongrel to the farm."

Gabriel went into his workshop where he kept his tools, and an old blacksmith's leg vice. There standing upright in the vice, with a file balanced as though grasped in the skeletonised hand, was the missing arm. Chuckling he called his Missus in to have a look.

The lads were late for dinner but they made up for it by helping Gabriel in his garden in the afternoon. Then after tea, and still chuckling about the arm in the vice, he walked back home with them. It was the sort of clear night when moonlight plays tricks with your vision. Walking past an open gate the lads saw a rabbit running across the bare pasture then vanish. Gabriel said, "It's just stopped, and because everything looks th' same colour in moonlight yer can't see it against th' grass."

Walking into the field Jack said, "We'll soon find out." Sure enough when he reached the spot where a rabbit had seemingly vanished it sprang up with such a startling scurry that Jack jumped back.

"Yer can't see anything on the ground but you can see it against the sky if you look upwards." Gabriel said. "So there'll be no poachers out with long nets tonight."

"What about shooting pheasants out of trees, can they see them against the sky?"

"Aye they can that lad."

The lads asked more questions but Gabriel remembered the man with a gun and he went quiet.

After a chat with Jimmy, Gabriel bid him and the lads good night and started to walk back down the lane towards home - and maybe the pub. Reaching the gate where he had waited for the poachers he was startled when the village constable stepped out. "Here you are then Gabriel, Tom said you'd be along to wait with me."

"How do yer mean - wait with yer?"

"For that poacher you saw with a gun; it's just the night for him to be out, so where is the best place to wait?"

"You wait where yer want - I'll wait in th' pub." And with that Gabriel made to go on, but the constable gripped his arm. "Tom's waiting further down the lane and you know the land better than me; I need you with me."

Muttering, Gabriel followed the constable into the field and directed him towards the bushes where he had hidden before. But the constable said, "Let's wait by the gate into that pasture in case he comes that way."

"If he does he'll have a surprise and he'll be in a hurry, because there's a young bull in with them cattle that's real nasty."

"How do you know what cattle are in which field?"

"Arr well; yer need to watch what goes on in the fields as well as on the road, an' that bull was with those heifers they moved in there yesterday - an' I tell yer he's a bad un."

So they moved behind Gabriel's bush and waited in complete silence. Fortunately he had put on a heavy coat and taken his blackthorn knob stick when he set out with the boys, although neither did anything for the icy feeling of fear that fluttered down his back.

An hour passed by and then they heard a bit of movement among the heifers. Suddenly the bull's bellow made them jump round and as they did a man came tumbling over the field gate and lay winded on their side of it. Gabriel saw the gun fall out of his hand as he fell and ran forward to pick it up . The policeman pinned the man to the ground. On the other side of the gate the bull bellowed in anger and pushed threateningly against it.

"Let's get away from that ugly beast's long horns," said Gabriel.

The poacher seemed to agree and was the first up the field with the constable hanging onto his arm and always looking over his shoulder.

Within a short time Tom had appeared, explaining that he had seen the man coming in their direction and followed him, but sensibly staying out of the bull's field. Gabriel grumbled, "I notice when there's a gun about, I'm there and yer somewhere else."

"It's just the luck of the draw; anyway we got him, didn't we."

"The constable's got him - an yer owe me a pint."

The three men walked their prisoner back to the village. Passing the pub, Gabriel said to Tom. "I'll have that pint now if yer don't mind?"

"After that bloody bull I could do with one as well." said the prisoner - the first words he had spoken.

"You'll have to settle for two nights in my cell because it will be Monday before you can face the magistrate."

"Arr, an' yer know whose pheasants yer were going to shoot, don't you - an' Monday's his bad day," Gabriel laughed.

"You might laugh now, you old bxxxxx, but when I get out I'll be back with my mates and we'll fix you."

"Eh why pick on me? I just tag a long with these two - an' I get the pellets - an' now I get the threats."

Giving the poacher a hefty push on towards the police house, the constable said. "If you do that the squire will put you inside for so long that you'll be too old to do any more damage when you come out."

"Yes and we'll know who to look out for in future." Tom said as he followed Gabriel into the pub.

The two men downed their pints in satisfaction. Tom would have bought a second but there was a group of four farmers having a pre-Christmas celebration and when they heard how Gabriel had helped to catch a poacher they each insisted on buying him a drink. The farmers had been in there a while and were in a jolly mood, the harvest had been good, the autumn work was well under way, and because each would have geese and chickens to pluck for the Christmas market this would be the last time they could meet before New Year. Life long friends, who farmed several miles out on different sides of the village, they met in the pub once a month for a get together.

Gabriel had noticed the four ponies in their traps, tied to the fence, as he and Tom walked in, but he thought no more about it until the farmers decided it was time to go. Gabriel was feeling the effects of his pints himself but the farmers were far more unsteady and he and Tom went out to help them. The moon was now hidden behind a cloud but the four farmers seemed to know which trap belonged to each. As Tom helped one very unsteady farmer up, he said, "I hope your pony knows its way home."

"He's.... never.... f-failed yet."

"Mine hasn't either." Another said in a slurred voice.

Knowing that the farmers would probably collapse on their trap seat and go to sleep relying on the ponies to take them safely home, Tom and Gabriel untied each pony and sent them on their way. Walking back to the pub Gabriel heard familiar laughter from behind the fence. "Come on out you lads, let's hear what yer've been up to now."

His two grandsons climbed over the fence with cheeky grins on their faces.

"Come on then, tell me what yer've done?"

"We swapped the ponies round, Grandad; we put them in to different traps."

Tom said. "That was a terrible thing to do, they'll end up in each other's yards and not know where they are. And they will be miles from home and too drunk to drive a strange pony to their own home."

"When I left yer at your father's I thought it was yer bedtime. What's he doing letting yer lads out at this time of night?"

"He doesn't know, he thinks we are in bed."

"Well yer'd better get home and get in bed before he does find out."

When the two men got back into the pub and told the story the locals thought it hilarious and there were lots of jokes about which bed each farmer might spend the night, and with whose wife.

"Maybe some of 'em 'll have the best night of their lives, eh?"

"There is one thing for sure none of them will find their way to the right bed tonight." Tom said to the laughing company.

The joke was certainly worth another round.

When they eventually came out Gabriel, looked up at the moon and said, "Err, I'm not taking that footpath across the fields, funny things happen to me in the dark. I think I'll just wander home along the lane, eh?"

When the spring buds were swelling on the trees George asked Gabriel for his daughter's hand. Despite the lad's turnip-sized pocket watch Gabriel had become quite fond of him and didn't hesitate to give his blessing. After her engagement Hannah seemed more than ever to live in a world of her own; on the few occasions she came out of it she would gush, "George will get promotion to be a stationmaster somewhere soon, and there will be a house with the job, and I shall be the stationmaster's wife."

In the new hierarchy created by the railway, a stationmaster was almost on a par with a bank manager. He was a man to be respected and his daughter would be such a man's wife. Gabriel cleared his throat, "Arr well that as maybe but yer not wed yet an' he's not a stationmaster, so help yer Mar with the pots."

That the oak leaves came out before the ash heralded a dry summer which, as it had already started, was helping to keep the weeds down among Gabriel's vegetables. It gave him time to relax and in that sort of mood one warm evening he sat on a gravestone near the back of the churchyard, lit his pipe, and waited for the barn owls to come hunting. He had already been up into Jim Slater's loft and seen the four young fluffy clad chicks, and knew the penalty the smallest would pay if food was scarce. He loved to watch the parents hunting in the dusk; their silent white wings reminded him of what he thought an angel might look like. But when the owls swooped the mouse below might not think it such an angel.

He was completely engrossed in the flight of one ghost-like bird when a voice said, "We knew we'd get you on your own sometime."

Old Gabriel sprang to his feet and turned to find the poacher and two mates closing in on him. They didn't see his blackthorn knob stick until he poked the attacking poacher in his stomach with the point and with the same move brought the knob end up to hit the second between his eyes. Just as the third hesitated the vicar walked across from the church. "Ah Gabriel, I hoped you would be here... Who are these men?"

"They just came for a chat, Vicar... I think they're leavin' now."

By this time the poacher and his mate were helping the third on to his feet and without a word they supported him across and out of the graveyard.

Feeling with his hand the sun's warmth still in the gravestone, the vicar sat down and said. "Are we going to sit and watch the barn owls for a while, Gabriel?"

Gabriel took his seat on the gravestone and muttered, "It's a funny thing, Vicar. When I wer' scared about being scared I wer' really scared, but when I'd no time to think about it, I wer' not scared at all."

"What are you on about, Gabriel?"

"Arr, nowt. It seems a peaceful night now Vicar."

The disturbance must have caused the barn owls to look for a quieter place to hunt because they didn't return. After a while the two men began to talk quietly.

"I've just come from the stationmaster's, do you know he's had a bad stroke?"

"Arr. Is he no better?"

"No, I doubt he will ever work again. The railway will probably retire him to a cottage somewhere and appoint a new stationmaster. In the meantime young George is acting stationmaster."

"Arr, he is that."

"Maybe they will appoint him but he will have to get married because they won't let an unmarried man into the station house. You could have a wedding on your hands, Gabriel."

"Arr, I reckon I'll need your help there vicar. I've not had a daughter married before."

"You know we will do anything to help. You know we haven't been blessed with children, Gabriel. Hannah has become very special to us since we've been here."

The leaves were beginning to fall off the trees when Gabriel walked proudly from his cottage to the church with his daughter on to his arm. The vicar's wife had brought out her old wedding dress, and with a few tucks and stitches it was a splendid fit. Hannah was a picture of health and happiness. Gabriel had dug out his old grey suit and he pushed back his bent old shoulders and walked proudly up to the altar to where George stood resplendent in his stationmaster's uniform. Gabriel now stepped back to join his Missus in her fine new dress on the front pew. He had had to sell more of his fruit and vegetables than he felt really prudent but with the money his Missus had bought the new dress and him a new shirt. And there weren't too many berries on the hedgerow trees so it might not be such a hard winter.

"Don't cry Missus, her'll only be down th' lane - an' we'll get by somehow, eh?"

. The winter was mild with only a few spells of hard frost and in between enough warmth to keep Gabriel's greens growing right through until late spring. His Missus kept the pears and apples sound by continually sorting out the occasional bad one; some of the best keepers, though wrinkled, were still edible by the end of June, which prompted Gabriel to say. "Arr yer've done a good job with this fruit Missus, without it things might have got a bit tight, eh?"

It was the vicar who was the troubled man now. Soon after he came to the village, a farmworker had lost his job on a farm on the fringe of the parish, and subsequently he was evicted from his cottage. The farmer claimed he was a loafer, only working three or four days each week. The worker claimed he was ill but the fact that he sought his medicine in the pub on his illness days undermined his case. Whatever the rights and wrongs of it, the vicar was brought into it because the husband, wife and three young children were to become homeless. He found them temporary accommodation, paying the rent from the poor fund.

Later he found some temporary work for the man, but the whole episode turned the vicar against the tied cottages. What he hadn't realized was that just about everyone was in a tied house with little or no security of tenure. Even the tenant farmers, although often on the same farm through several generations, could be turned off their farm, and out of their house, at the whim of the landlord. In turn their farm tenancy contracts stated that they could only sub-let their farm cottages to an active farmworker. Most of the workers on the estate, from the gardener to the gamekeeper, lived in a house that went with the job;

even the vicar himself lived under the same conditions. Perhaps that was why he started to campaign against the tied cottage system?

At the next meeting with the squire the vicar said, "Sir Henry I am deeply troubled by the conditions your workers live under. They can lose their job and be turned out of their cottage at little more than a week's notice and your tenant farmers treat their workers the same way, seemingly without any regard to their future welfare."

The squire gave him a long searching look before replying. "You've got a nerve, Vicar, when your own employee, old Gabriel, is in a tied cottage. I rent the cottage to the church and the church rents the cottage to Gabriel strictly as part of his employment with you."

Shocked by his own ignorance the vicar took his leave. But having already complained to various people in the parish about the evils of the tied cottage he felt compelled to take some action. A visit to the land agent in the estate's office gave him a surprising way out because the agent explained that the estate was prepared to sell the occasional cottage on the fringe of the village if it was no longer needed for an estate worker, or if it might require expensive repairs in the near future.

Gabriel couldn't believe it when the vicar came to offer him the chance to buy his own cottage for £100. "Where will we get £100 from Missus, eh?"

When his Missus didn't provide an answer he worried about it through the afternoon, then on the way to the pub, and then, after a pint or two, on the way to see his lad Jimmy. "What does think, Jimmy, they're offering me my cottage for £100. Where can I find that, eh?"

Jimmy and Beth, his wife, exchanged looks for a few moments before Jimmy replied, "We might be able to help you there Dad; we haven't told you before but Beth has had a small inheritance. Maybe we could buy the cottage and let you have the tenancy and then some day in the future it would be there for us."

There were weeks of discussion between themselves and later with the landlord's agents before it was settled. The fact that it would need re-thatching in two or three years time didn't stop Gabriel and Jimmy and their wives from becoming property owners. The surprising thing was that when they got the deeds they included an additional 2 acres adjacent to Gabriel's garden bed in the corner of Jim Slater's field. Not that Jim had ever farmed it. Gabriel had thought that was because it needed to be drained and have the thorns and briars cleared, but, no, it seems it had always belonged to the cottage.

When the news of the cottage sale spread through the village it caused uproar. Very few agreed with the vicar, most had grown up with the tied cottage as a way of life and were incensed that Gabriel could now stop working for the church and still enjoy his cottage. Most villagers were adamant that the countryside couldn't run without workers being on hand. Apart from the railway there was no transport other than horse or foot and as most couldn't afford a horse they had to be in walking distance of their employment.

Over a pint in the pub Tom said to Gabriel. "The squire has done it on purpose. This estate couldn't run without tied cottages, everyone knows it bar the vicar."

"Arr and now he knows it too, but I've got my cottage so I reckon it turned out all right, eh?"

Gabriel and Jimmy were soon planning how they could drain the 2 acres; it would mean digging a deep drain alongside one of Jim Slater's fields but Gabriel was convinced that if he could bring the land into production he would be able to keep a cow. Even his Missus was excited at the thought of producing their own milk and homemade butter.

Jim Slater agreed to let them dig a drain across his field but only through the winter months when there was no crop, which created a problem because Jimmy could only help with the digging in an evening and of course in the winter months it was dark well before he had finished work on the farm.

In the meantime Hannah, who walked up to visit her parents on a couple of afternoons each week, was showing some expansion of her own. The baby was born in September and from then on Gabriel tried to pretend that he wasn't thrilled to see his grand-daughter on each visit. Unless there was a grave to dig, work was slack in the churchyard through the winter months and there wasn't too much to do on the casual gardening side, which meant that most days he could put in a few hours digging the new drain.

One warm December afternoon Hannah pushed the pram with one hand and carried a can of hot tea in the other across the garden to Gabriel. She left her father chuckling at the baby and went back to chat to her mother. He was still making cooing noises when Tom walked quietly up behind him. "You'll never get that drain dug if you spend the afternoon talking to your granddaughter."

Gabriel jumped round spluttering with embarrassment but Tom saved him by saying, "No, I envy you, I missed having children and seeing you now I miss even more having grandchildren."

"Arr, an they are a great comfort to me in me old age too; mind you them two twins have given me a bit of hassle but they seem to have quieted down now they're working full-time."

"Yes I saw young Rob walking back from the station last night, he seems to be enjoying his work. Anyway it's my old age I have come to talk about, not yours. I'm getting too old to go chasing after poachers in the middle of the night so I'm thinking about retiring. Well not fully but the Squire has got a little cottage free in the village. It's only one up, one down with a lean-to kitchen but if we move into that the Squire can take on a new head keeper and I can help him out a bit part-time. What do you think Gabriel?"

"I don't know why yer worried - isn't it usually me that meets the poachers, eh? Yes, I should take it Tom, yer've done more than yer share, eh?"

Gabriel poured Tom his last cup of tea and watched him drink it while he lit his pipe. The baby watched the smoke curling upwards, cooed a bit more and went to sleep, so the two old men smiled indulgently and walked along the side of the drain.

It had become a tradition for Jimmy and his family to share Christmas day with his parents. Gabriel always reared a few cock chickens and his Missus plucked and dressed one of the largest for the big day; so this year they were surprised when one of the twins called in to tell them that his Mum and Dad were going to visit Beth's sister for Christmas. But they could come for dinner on the Sunday before. So the cock chicken lost his head a few days earlier than expected and was in the oven roasting away while they were at morning service.

Afterwards the family all walked back from the church together and whilst his missus took the chicken out of the oven and put some vegetables on to boil, Gabriel asked his grandsons about their jobs. Rob was an engineering apprentice and Jack was working on the home farm. Then Hannah walked in followed by George carrying the baby. Gabriel had no idea they were coming and was overwhelmed to see all his family crowded together in his small parlour. He had hardly got over his surprise when a clatter of horses hoofs drew him outside, to be met there by her ladyship. "There you are Gabriel, I just called to wish you all a very happy Christmas in your new home."

"Well me Lady, thanks to the vicar it is me own home now."

"Tosh - the vicar had nothing to do with it. When we were discussing Tom's retirement Sir Henry said that it was time we resolved your future as well. When that silly young vicar started interfering in the estate's business we thought we would teach him a lesson at the same time. Anyway you must have been thrilled to hear Jimmy's news."

"What news? He's only told us that he's going to visit Beth's sister."

Her ladyship passed him his usual Christmas envelope with a cheery smile and just returned to her two-in-hand carriage. The groom called "walk on" and Gabriel saluted her as she smiled once more through the window. He turned back into the house with the question still on his mind. "Jimmy what's this news her wer' on about?"

"We were going to tell you when we were all sitting down. I've left the farm so we are going to visit Beth's sister before I start my new job in the New Year."

"What are yer on about, yer've said nowt to me about another job?"

It was obvious from the look on everyone's face bar Gabriel's that they all knew something very pleasing. Jimmy in particular stood proudly in front of his father and said, "From the first of January I will be the bailiff at the home farm."

The whole affair was too much for Gabriel; when his Missus put the chicken on the table his hands shook so much he couldn't slice it up so he held out the knife, "Here yer are Missus, yer'll make a better job than me, eh?"

Below the Waterwheel

Emma worked quietly, completely absorbed in the movement of her foot on the treadle of the sewing machine. As she fed the two hems towards the chattering needle she marvelled how lucky it was for her that her aunt owned a dress shop in town. Although the villagers and local farming families brought in some work, it was spasmodic. Each Wednesday afternoon she listened for the sound of her aunt's hired pony and trap clattering along the quiet country lane outside.

These weekly visits, bringing orders for new dresses or others to be altered, were the mainstay of her living. The steady, if meagre, income allowed Emma to work from home and still care for her sister. Afternoon tea with her aunt also brought news from outside the quiet little village and brightened her week.

Since the death of her father, Emma's life had been dominated by the need to care for her young sister Molly. Not that Molly was ever ill. On the contrary, she had a healthy complexion, a tall slim, attractive body and an angelic face. It was only when you looked into her large blue eyes that you realised that there was something wrong, they seemed to be vacant, to lack comprehension. All that her father ever said was"We nearly lost her - the midwife couldn't cope and when I ran for the Doctor he was out on another call."

The strain of that birth took so much out of her mother that she had very poor health afterwards and had died when Molly was only nine. From then on Emma had helped her father bring up her beautiful young sister. Then when Molly was in her mid-teens he had had a heart attack and Emma had been left to manage on her own.

As Emma snipped the cotton and turned the dress she realised that Molly seemed very quiet in the other room. When calling out to her illicited no reply Emma went through the little cottage to look for her. She wasn't there and the door was open. Emma wasn't too concerned and took her time to look round the garden before walking along the lane. This really was a quiet little Cheshire village where strangers were rare, doors were seldom locked and all the locals knew Molly.

About a hundred yards up the lane a footpath left the road to cut across a small meadow to the brook side. It then followed up the brook through a wooded valley for about 400 yards before crossing a small field to the water mill. When she leaned over the stile she was relieved to see Molly's small footprint in the soft ground on the field's side. She was relieved because her fiancé Ben was the miller.

Although Ben's father was still alive he was so crippled with rheumatism nowadays that Ben had returned home to run the Mill. Ben was good with Molly, she responded to him more than to anyone else. "Yes, she'll be all right if she's gone to the mill," Emma said to herself with a smile. Without the need to rush, but glad of the excuse to go to visit Ben, Emma returned to the cottage to finish the last seam before slipping on her coat and walking shoes.

The brook was up which meant that Ben would be milling, she thought. As the millstones ground the whole building would be rumbling and creaking with the power and movement of the water wheel. Emma remembered the first time that this had happened - that Molly had disappeared. She had run all the way only to find Molly helping Ben to weigh up the sacks of freshly ground flour. Well, she presumed that it was Ben, because although she had heard of his return home she had not seen him since her school days. Emma had stopped in the doorway watching in amazement how Molly was responding to Ben's instructions, pouring some flour into the top of one sack and then standing watching while he tied up the neck of the sack before lifting it off the scales. When Ben lifted the next sack onto the scales he said, "it's too heavy, take a scoopful out...." and Molly did just that.

Through the previous years Emma had had several hopeful suitors, but always mindful that there was Molly to care for, she had discouraged them. Ben couldn't be discouraged in quite the same way because Molly kept escaping and when Emma found her she was in the mill doing some simple task on Ben's instructions.

Ben began to use the footpath in the other direction, visiting Emma and Molly in the dark winter evenings. Although both girls were pleased to see him and him them, he soon left no doubt about his special interest in Emma. He and Emma would sit by the fire late, talking and exploring each other's thoughts. But when Molly wanted Ben's attention he did not seem to mind. He would show her how to do simple drawings or get her to talk a little about her day. Emma was amazed how Molly responded, putting words into sentences in a way that she had never managed before.

Ben's rugged face and understanding smile had won Emma's heart on that first day. Now his skill with Molly had broken down her traditional resistance and she had gladly accepted his proposal and fixed the day for their marriage later that summer.

Following the footpath out from the trees below the mill race pool, Emma was startled to see the local policeman David Smith and one or two others. David had been a close friend of Ben's in their school days but he had been stationed for eight years further across Cheshire. He had been thrilled to return to the village as its constable and renew his friendship with Ben through these last few months.

David turned quickly and came to her. Gripping her by her shoulders he said, "Don't go any further, there's been an accident."

"Who?"

"It's Molly! We've sent for the doctor but I'm sorry Emma.... I am afraid there's nothing he can do!" He held Emma firmly as she struggled shouting, "Let me go to her."

"It isn't nice; she was in the water, and I think she may have come through the wheel. Her face is crushed and most of her clothes have gone. It's better you don't see her."

She screamed in sudden awareness. "Where's Ben?"

"We don't know! No one can find him."

Ben's mother came down and she and one of the other village wives led Emma up to the Mill house. David was left to get on with his police work. He searched the mill without finding a trace of Ben or anything that might suggest Molly had got entangled in the water wheel. When he returned the village doctor was examining the body carefully. Taking David on one side he said, "I think that she's been hit with something heavy, perhaps a brick. Anyway, there looks to be traces of brick dust in the wound."

There were only three telephones in the village. The doctor had one, the village post office had the second, and now David had been provided with the third. He already had mixed feelings about the phone because his Sergeant found it too easy to bellow instructions down it. That the Sergeant always shouted amused David. This time though, after David had made his report, when the Sergeant shouted that the Chief Inspector was at the local town's police station, David's grin froze. The Chief was a city man with little knowledge of country people or their ways and in the past David had managed to provoke him with his too easy demonstration of country knowledge.

When the Chief Inspector came on the phone saying, "I'm taking charge," David just said, "Yes, sir," and a knot turned in his stomach. He barked out a list of instructions. "Don't move the body, keep the doctor there, don't let any of the witnesses go..... and leave the questions to me!"

David repeated, "Yes, sir."

David's colleagues joked that the only bright side about the Chief getting a motor car was that it often either wouldn't start or was broke down. If it started this time it would take the most part of an hour for him to motor out. Which gave David just time to talk to Emma again. But she couldn't add anything to help him.

After searching the three storey mill again, he was still very puzzled. In the top loft five sacks of wheat stood ready to be poured into the chute leading down to the grinding stones situated on the middle floor, but no flour had come through from the stones down the chute onto the bottom floor. Normally there was a winding handle to lift open the heavy sluice gate, now it was jammed wide open with a crowbar and the handle seemed to be missing. David knew it was opened too wide, the water would have rushed out so fast that the wheel would have been driven at such a crazy speed that it would have damaged the stones - particularly without grain flowing down between them, they would have ground against each other until the millpool ran out of water. Ben wouldn't let that happen, would he? He walked round the now empty mill pool still without finding a trace of Ben.

Returning to where the body lay covered on the bank, he could see where Ben had recently done some work at the bottom end of the tail race pool. After it turned the big wooden wheel the rush of water came down the tail race to cut deep into the ground forming a clear fast flowing pool. This pool had served as the swimming pool in David and Ben's school days. He remembered how they had persuaded Ben's father to tip a cartload of old bricks across the tail end to raise the water level and give them a bit more depth in which to swim.

Washed clean by the running water those bricks had lain there through the intervening years. A few days before when David walked the meadow footpath he noticed that the flow of water had cut into the bank, washing a narrow channel around the side of the bricks, between them and the bank. The other side of the pool was protected by a steep tree-covered bank which rose from the water's edge some eighty feet before flattening into fertile fields above. He could see that Ben had thrown some of those bricks into the channel.

When the Chief Inspector arrived he soon came to a conclusion. "The poor girl's clothes have been ripped off in a sexual frenzy... and when she struggled the attacker must have snatched up a brick and hit her."

David asked. "But who?"

The Inspector swiftly replied, "The Miller is missing, what's his name? Ben! Yes he must have run away, shocked at what he'd done."

David's protestations were dismissed with a sharp, "I tell you - find Ben and we've found our killer!"

Although the post-mortem confirmed how Molly had died, there was no evidence of a sexual assault. When a search of the area failed to yield further clues or anything of Ben, the Chief Inspector was even more resolutely convinced of his theory. Through the next few days David tried several times to point out that the the five sacks of wheat standing at the top of the chute, the jammed sluice gate and the fact that Ben loved Molly were all completely against it. Loved was the wrong word to use. The Chief just got more angry. "Loved, loved, of course he did! She was attractive, young and devoted to him. He loved her alright, it's just that he couldn't keep his hands off her."

David had to tell Emma what the official police line was. She was so distraught that she tried to hit him, flaying with her arms in angry disbelief and disgust.

David knew in his heart she was right and went back again to reason with his boss but the Chief Inspector only got angry again, "Smith you are supposed to mix with the villagers to aid your police work, not to get so involved with them that you can't see the facts."

David protested, "I know Ben, he wouldn't have killed her. He wouldn't kill anyone"

The Chief almost exploded. "Where is he then? It's time you got back to some real police work in the town. This country nonsense is not good for you!"

Ben's father managed to go to Molly's funeral, where he stood in obvious distress by the open grave. Emma stepped up alongside him and held his arm. She said quietly, "It wasn't Ben... I know it wasn't Ben!" Ben's father smiled weakly and a tear showed as he gripped her hand. Suddenly the old man's head sagged and he just seemed to crumble slowly to the floor. People rushed forward to pull him away from the graveside.

When weeks went by without any news of Ben, Emma began to despair. The villagers, growing tired and embarrassed of her protests that Ben was innocent, now began to avoid her. To most people, Ben had been found guilty without a trial. She did try to visit and help with Ben's father, who had not been well since his collapse at the graveside, but the murder had destroyed the happy relationship she had previously enjoyed with Ben's mother.

The neighbouring farmer, Huw Cornthwaite, who farmed the fields on the bank just across the brook from the mill, and who had been a previous suitor of Emma, again began to seek her out. She had never responded to his advances. It was not that he was bad looking; but something about him just repulsed her. After the funeral he called at the cottage several times, expressing sympathy. But when he made the mistake of suggesting that it had to be Ben who had killed Molly, Emma ran from him in horror.

Emma's aunt as always came to her rescue. She told Emma that because her health was failing she found she could no longer cope with the shop and she pleaded for her to come to town and help her. It worked, of course. Emma found that she enjoyed meeting the customers in the bustle of the busy shop. Her aunt was not as ill as she had made out but she did take the welcome opportunity to take more time off, leaving the shop in Emma's capable hands.

Within a month of the murder David was moved to Altrincham. There his talent and dedication soon showed and he was transferred to the plain-clothed side of police work. Occasionally he visited his parents who still lived just outside the old village, but the uncertainty of what had happened to Ben and Molly spoiled such visits for him.

He also called at the shop a few times to talk with Emma. As much as he enjoyed talking to her - and she seemed pleased to see him - each visit seemed to trigger the agony locked in her mind. She couldn't help herself. "Ben didn't do it, he couldn't harm her, I know he couldn't. You're all wrong!" However much David told her that he believed her, the fact was the Chief didn't, and he was the police! After three or four visits, David didn't go again.

As the time went by David sat his sergeant's exams and was delighted when he passed first time. With a little more money in his pocket he decided that he needed to take up a hobby again, and another detective inspector reintroduced him to a childhood passion - fishing, fly-fishing to be exact. For a man with his country background and his interest in nature, fly-fishing was the ideal way to relax. Soon he found all the tension and excitement of police work could be forgotten as he stalked a rising trout along the banks of the River Bollin.

He thought of the mill stream back at home - and he had promised to visit his parents soon. How he would like to take his new fly rod along those banks and fish the places he had known as a worm-fishing boy. He didn't know if it was the fishing, or the old village or his parents, but there was an overwhelming need for him to return.

Emma heard the sad news that Ben's father had died and she decided she must take a break from the shop to return to the village. She had not been back to her cottage since moving to town two years before, so the first day was taken up with dusting and cleaning, but on her second day, the day before the funeral, Emma was up early and determined to visit Ben's mother, however difficult it seemed to be. Although they had been good friends before Ben disappeared the emotion of meeting again was heartbreaking. Even more heartbreaking was to see that the caring old woman seemed to have worn herself out nursing her husband this past two years, and Emma had not been able to be there to help her.

After a cup of tea, which eased the tension, Ben's Mother explained that they had never worked the mill again since that dreadful day. Engine-driven grinding machines were already taking the trade away from the slower water mills, even before Ben's death, she said - she had been convinced from the beginning that he was dead. After Ben had returned home he had been supplementing the mill's income by doing metal work for local farmers. She had decided that, after her husband's funeral, she was going into Derbyshire to stay with her sister. Because she had neither set foot in the mill nor in Ben's workshop since his death, she asked Emma if she would be kind enough to go and look round, to see if everything was alright to be left.

When Emma walked into the mill it was incredible; everything was as it had been on that dreadful day two years before. The sluice gate was still jammed open. Now that the water had been diverted, grass and weeds grew round the sides of the empty mill pool. On the ground floor, the weighing room, where Molly had helped Ben so many times, stood cobwebbed and empty. More cobwebs and dust covered the stairs and the once vital grinding stones. At the top of the stairs the five bags of grain still stood unclaimed by the chute.

Images of the two people she had loved so much crowded Emma's thoughts as she walked across the weed-covered yard to Ben's small workshop. He had converted what had been a small brick loosebox equipping it with a forge, anvil and all the tools necessary to do repairs to the mill machinery. And the locals had soon made use of his skills.

Emma stood inside, picturing Ben's strong brown arm resting the red-hot steel on the anvil while he struck it with a heavy hammer. Suddenly she froze. On the anvil was the rusted handle to the sluice gate; she could see the hammer marks where Ben had been reshaping the head. If Ben had been repairing it, then it wasn't lost. And if it wasn't lost then Ben wouldn't have needed to lever the sluice gate open with a crowbar. She turned and stared out through the window. She was looking out over the tail race pool and into the wooded bank beyond. If Ben had looked up from his work he would have seen Molly coming along the meadow-side footpath. He would have seen whoever attacked her... He would have rushed out to help! Yes......

Suddenly Emma grasped an old spade from by the door and was running towards the bottom end of the millrace pool. She knew where Ben was! The day Ben vanished she had also seen that those bricks had been moved but she had thought nothing of it..... until now. As she relived that day, she remembered clearly that they had not been moved the day before.

Two years of mud and debris had filled the holes between them almost cementing them in to place. Sobbing with rage and frustration she struggled to dig the bricks out but they seem wedged together and then she heard a splash as someone jumped the brook behind her.

The funeral had given David the final excuse he needed to visit his parents - and do that bit of fly fishing with his new green-heart fly rod, on the brook of his youth. When he got down to the water he soon found that it was difficult to cast a fly line among the many alders and ash that lined the brook banks. As he tried to cast sideways beneath them, David fished his way up stream towards the meadow by Emma's cottage, without taking a fish. Now remembering the open meadow by the mill pool pulling him, David walked through the wood towards it. At the end of the wood he was surprised to see movement on the far bank high up above the waterside. It looked like Huw Cornthwaite and he was hiding behind a tree watching something down by the brook. David was intrigued and walked closer...... when Cornthwaite leapt from behind the tree and ran down the steep bank David ran forward instinctively, his heart pounding.

He now saw Emma frantically trying to dig; and then Cornthwaite splashing across the brook to snatch the spade out of her hand. He ran as fast as he could but was still a few yards short when he saw Cornthwaite raise the spade high above Emma's head and shout, "You stupid bitch. You couldn't leave it alone, could you... you silly bitch!"

David's anguished shout made Cornthwaite spin round to face him, and without breaking stride David drove his right fist on to the point of the farmer's jaw. He was out cold - but a pair of handcuffs in David's top coat seemed very appropriate to him and he reflexly fitted them.

Emma, who had stood frozen to the spot throughout it all, now started to break down. When David caught hold of her she pointed down at the bank, whispering hoarsely, "I know where Ben is! David, I know where he is! The sluice gate handle. It wasn't lost, Ben was mending it... in his workshop! He saw what happened. The bricks were moved that day!"

David realised suddenly that the narrow channel would just hold a body. He turned to Emma. "The sluice gate hadn't been opened to hide Molly's murder - it was to wash over the bricks to hide Ben's burial."

He looked into Emma's eyes, kissed her gently on the forehead, and picked up the spade. He knew what he would find beneath those bricks. He also knew in his heart that, whatever happened in the future, this brave woman must become his wife.

The Young Ploughman

I sometimes walk along the banks of the River Dane near my home looking to cut shanks for walking sticks. One bank is so steep that I wasn't brave enough to cut a nice blackthorn shank growing right on the brink. The near vertical 100 foot bank is broken by narrow grassy ledges on which trees cling perilously to the steep side. At one place, where an old grassy path ran at an angle from top to bottom, previous generations of local lads sat on thick sacks using it as a hair-raising dry sled run.

Retired farmer Arthur Malkin tells how once a youth was ploughing on the flat field along the brink of that bank when his team went over the edge taking the plough with them. Once over there was no way they could stop until they hit the river some 100 foot below.

After he had ploughed a single furrow round the field to mark out the headland, the young ploughman lined up both his two-horse team and the plough so that they faced directly across the field. He was so proud; it was the first time his father had let him plough a field on his own.

Leaving the horses to rest he strode out towards the far side, thrilled that he was at last old enough to live out his dream to be a ploughman. About two thirds of the way across he paused to push a stick into the turf with a bit of rag tied on so that he would be able see it clearly from across the field. The youth walked on until he came to the edge of the field, where he paused to let the breeze fill his lungs with the salty tang of the sea.

On this headland there was neither fence nor tree, just a steep drop of some thirty feet down to a narrow ledge running along the very edge of the cliff, which, was formed by wave smoothed rocks and towered upright some seventy feet from the foreshore below.

Gulls argued among the boulders strewn along the beach beneath him, while others wheeled and swooped in noisy refrain. To his left a small rocky bay formed a sheltered pool where at low tide he and other village children swam in the warmth of the summer.

But he wasn't a child now. He was a man with a man's work to do, so he turned back and placed his second marker in line with his first and the team. In his mind he heard his Dad, "It's easier to line up your markers with the team than struggle to do it the other way round."

Back with the horses he took one rein and a plough handle in each hand; now all he had to do was to drive his team towards those markers across the field. "Just keep your eye on them," his Dad had said, "don't look away and don't look back." But the experienced old horses strode towards the markers without his guidance. When he was nearing the far side he felt a growing pride, confident that it would be a straight furrow.

But what was that, down there on the beach, to the left of the far marker? It was a girl sitting among the rocks by the small bay. At first he could only see her raven black hair but with each step, as the horses took him closer, he could see more. Next the ivory white of her naked shoulders came into view and then down - until he could see almost to her waist. "Woe! Woe," called the youth to his team floundering on the very brink of the headland. "Back! Back," he called, desperately tugging backwards at the plough to give the two powerful shires room to turn back to the furrow. Alas when he did manage to turn his team and plough round there was a distinct bend in the last ten yards.

At a time when only the most brazen of girls gave a boy more than a glimpse of her ankles the youth couldn't help but look again. She turned her head to look up at him, their eyes met and a shy smile spread across her angelic face. Flustered and blushing with embarrassment, he turned back to his plough calling to the two old horses, "Walk-on".

Turning the team round on the gate side of the field as quickly as he could, the youth urged them back faster and ever faster until flecks of lather glistened on their flanks. But when he got to the headland and looked down to the rocky pool again she was gone.

He worked on through until the early afternoon, the seagulls wheeling above his head and diving down behind the plough for worms. He stopped several times to let his eyes search among the rocks. Alas there was no one there. The two old horses, both older than the youth now working them, could only work a very short day. "Just teach my lad how to plough," the old farmer had said that morning, patting their necks affectionately, "and then you two can retire out to grass."

The following day the seagulls were waiting in a great flock when the youth returned to the field. When his team came close to the cliff headland his heart skipped a beat when the raven hair came into view again. As the powerful horses strode with the plough towards the headland he saw ivory white shoulders and.... "Woe! Woe!" Again the two horses almost walked over the edge of the drop. "Back! Back!" he called, desperately tugging at the plough handles.

Shaken by the near disaster, the youth struggled to turn the plough. Now he had to hold and balance it up off the ground so that it run on its front wheel while the horses walked along the headland, passing yesterday's furrows, before turning to plough back across the field. "Never wrap the reins round your wrists, if a horse takes fright you'll be dragged of your feet before you can blink," his Dad often told him. But he couldn't hold the reins and the plough off the ground at the same time. "Anyway these horses have never ran away. They know more about ploughing than I do," he said to himself. And so, wrapping a reign round each wrist, he balanced the plough up clear of the ground and called "walk-on" again.

But he couldn't resist glancing down; it was just as the girl turned sideways to look up. He saw the bright smile on her face, the sea spray sparkling on the white of her shoulder. Then, when she lifted her arm to beckon to him he saw the full upward curve of her firm young breast. His knees went weak, his arms sagged and the point of the plough bit into the tough old turf. Catching at an angle, the plough handles were thrown to the right, which caused his left arm to tighten on that reign.

The outside horse, turning in response, stopped, trembling on the brink, while the inside horse, pulled round by the same move, couldn't stop and bumped into her. Before he could even shout she was over the edge sliding, kicking and dragging the other after her. The plough handles were wrenched from his hands to bounce down after them. But the reins were still round his wrists.

Miraculously on the ledge of the cliff edge, the horses seemed to momentarily halt their fall. The reins had jerked the youth like a conker on a string to land on the ledge to their left. In that split second, as he skidded to a jarring stop he was aware of the struggling horses, of the plough bouncing down towards them. But his eyes were on the rocky bay below where there was a flash of ivory white and - although he heard the sickening thud of the plough hitting the horses and their screams of terror as they were knocked over the cliff edge - he saw a tail fin rise from the water, splash down once and vanish beneath the waves. And the reins were still round his wrists.

Parish Records, Gawsworth and North Rode

The parishes of Gawsworth and North Rode are undulating and attractive rolling countryside. Much of Gawsworth is light or even sandy soil with deep patches of peat in the lower areas on many fields, whereas although North Rode has some of the same type of soil, it is described in the Cheshire Gazetteer of 1850 as 'being mostly cold and wet'.

The banks along the River Dane Valley, which form one boundary of North Rode, are in places very steep and where tributaries run into the Dane they too can be in quite deep sided valleys. Cow Brook is one such tributary that was dammed to form North Rode pool, with the drive to the Manor House going across the top of the dam. The overflow runs into the top of a stone basin and in its early years the pressure of water down that narrow stone channel created a fountain shooting some 40 feet high. I never saw it working but I believe it was spectacular and although the fountain no longer works the lake's overflow of water still issues out with such force that it has created a deep basin at the foot of the dam.

In the days when each village had its own policeman they would cycle round their patch calling on different farmers for a cup of tea and a chat. One local bobby was cycling through the park one dark night when he met a gang of poachers as they too crossed over the dam. There followed a bit of a struggle and the policeman was thrown down the deep embankment into that basin. Fortunately he wasn't seriously hurt, but he never found his helmet. I doubt if you could persuade a modern policeman to cycle through there on a dark winter's night.

Although the drive is private it is possible to drive through and out of the other end without going near to the Manor House; and not all those who do so go just for the scenery. In the early years, before there was the means of transport to take fresh milk into Manchester, cheese was made on almost every dairy farm but not every dairy farmer made a good cheese. Milk at the wrong temperature or certain weeds grazed by cows could taint the flavour of a cheese, even the pretty meadow buttercup if too dominant could give the cheese an unpleasant flavour.

Whatever the reason a cartload of rejected cheeses was dumped off the dam one dark night. Cheeses were bobbing down Cow Brook and into the Dane for days afterwards.

Life was still very feudal in the Gawsworth Parish around 1900. Except for three farms, Lord Harrington owned the entire Parish and most of Bosley. Gawsworth on its own is the second largest Parish in Cheshire. Yet strangely the much smaller Parish of North Rode, lying directly between the other two, was in separate ownership and had been for centuries. I had to go back to the 12th century to find the family name Bigod linked to both estates. North Rode has passed through many different families through the intervening years, among them the Earls of Oxford and the Crewes of Crewe. Near the end of the 18th century Lord Crewe sold the estate to John Daintry whose family held the property until recent times.

Gawsworth village consisted mostly of small farms dotted along the roadsides. There would be perhaps five or ten acres and on them the wife and family did most of the work whilst the husband worked on the larger farms in the parish or for the landlord on his estate. The cropping on those large farms was more arable than now with a lot of winter wheat grown. The repeal of the Corn Laws in the second half of the 19th century caused a prolonged farm slump, and with it came a gradual change to more pastural farming.

Gawsworth's Parish Council meeting was held on December 14th 1894 when the Rector John Penrose was elected chairman. The membership consisted of one boot and shoemaker, one gentleman and six farmers. The clerk was to be paid £2.00 per year. They scheduled a second meeting for 25th March but before then they fitted in two extra meetings. They had really caught the 'politics bug'. But the clerk could not take the strain and became ill.

Gawsworth Parish Council took over the work of the old Vestry Committee. This was a self-elected group that, as its name suggests, met in the Church vestry. Its work had been mostly amongst the poor, administering various charities, of which the Moss Terrace Property charity was the most important in Gawsworth. The funds from this were divided between the school, where they appointed a manager, and the poor. When the Parish Council took the charity work over there were about twenty needy people listed by name. They were helped mostly by the gift of coal, up to 25 hundredweights provided annually for the most needy.

The business of the new Parish Council was more varied, but with that many farmer members it soon became mainly agricultural. The gentleman and the shoemaker soon had enough and were replaced by two more farmers. Among its many roles the Parish Council appointed the Parish mole-catcher - but presumably each tenant paid him a fee.

One eye-catching entry was the demand to the County Council that, "They take action to deal with the large flocks of sparrows and green linnets infesting the County." At a later meeting they went further and demanded that the County Council should pay for the destruction of sparrows and linnets at the rate of 3d per dozen heads and 1d per dozen eggs.

A report from the District Surveyor was made at the request of the Parish Council, for a new road through Shellow Farm to North Rode. The estimated cost from the main road through to Rode Green, a distance of about ³/₄ of a mile, was £255. Although its opening date was not recorded I guess that it was about 1906. Mr Jas Hague had by then become the Chairman. A plaster cast of Queen Victoria was bought for the school on her Diamond Jubilee - just before she died.

Planning to celebrate the coronation of King Edward VII took a sub committee and many hours of council time. The result was that 400 people sat down to a meal followed by a sports evening for a total cost of £52.

Between 1910 and 1919 Mr Jas Hague was still in the chair and names like Harry Lomas and John Trueman appeared in reports, farming names still active in the parish today. The Council minutes were still dominated with farming issues. Moles were getting out of hand so they appealed to his Lordship's agent to put pressure on those tenants who were failing to catch the moles on their farms. Although it doesn't say what the pressure was I think we can presume it was to get the tenant farmers to pay the mole-catcher for his last year's work, then he would catch on the farm again the next year.

Another sub committee was formed to celebrate George V's coronation in 1910. Tea for 300 adults cost 2/- per head.

The first mention of Gawsworth's dangerous crossroads called them, "A death trap for motorists" (it still is today). And a proposal for new council houses came forward.

After 1920 a new rule was made that chairmen should only serve for two years and this brought new names forward, among them Richard Thornicroft, another with a grandson still farming in the parish. The council house building site was decided on and a War Memorial planned with trees to be planted round it.

An outbreak of foot and mouth took the council's attention. Letters were written to the Ministry of Agriculture on the issues of tithes and land rents. The Parish Council had to approve each new council house tenant. They still had two meetings each month in winter, which were held in the Clerk's cottage.

Between 1930 and 1935 the Clerk, Mr S.P. Bayley, was paid £16-7-0. The first street light in Gawsworth was erected at the crossroads in 1931 and in 1932 they agreed to have water laid onto Gawsworth from the Trent Bank reservoir. The cost of the four-inch main was £1876. Times were getting hard and the Clerk's salary was reduced to £15 per annum. The celebration for George V's Silver Jubilee in 1935 included mugs for the children and tea for the over 65s at a cost of 1/6 per head.

In 1937 local papers tell how the playing fields were purchased from Mrs Bayley (the Clerk's widow) for £350. They make it clear that she could have had much more from a builder.

More Gawsworth Stories

The fact that apart from the chairman there was just a boot and shoemaker, one gentleman and six farmers serving on the council in 1894, reveals how the village has changed in 100 years. There is only one farmer on the Parish Council today. Agriculture took up most of the Council's time in those early years to the extent that the boot and shoemaker and the gentleman, perhaps tiring of the mainly farming agenda, soon retired. It is still a large farming parish but if agriculture comes on the agenda today it is usually because it smells or leaves mud on the roadway.

The term 'gentleman' is often found in documents from that period so where did this so-called gentleman fit into village hierarchy. Many Cheshire villages were owned by absentee landlords. Gawsworth was no exception and it was Lord Harrington who owned most of the property. The landlord's agent was a real power in the life of any parish; farmers, craftsmen and villagers lived in awe of him. To make his life easier the agent often let some of the smaller or more basic properties to a gentleman who in turn was responsible for sub-letting to the occupying tenants. The gentleman set and collected the rent from those properties and in turn he paid a proportion of it as his rent to the agent, who in turn handed it over to the landlord. The tenant? Well he just doffed his hat to 'the lot of 'em'. The term gentleman was also used to describe someone of independent means, who did not fit into the traditional village hierarchy.

In the late 1920's the Parish Council met in the home of the Clerk, Mr S.P. Bayley. The £16-7-0 per annum he drew for his services, we presume also covered the meeting taking place in his home.

I was told by the late Ernest Bayley, the Clerk's son, that when meeting in the small but comfortable cottage, the Council members took turns to bring a bottle of whisky to the meeting. It wasn't opened until after the business was over but the tradition was that the bottle had to be emptied before they dispersed. Now I have not discovered what size the bottle was but reading the minutes I did learn that at some meetings there was as few as four or five members present. Guess the size of the bottle and do your own calculations.

During this period Mr Jas Hague, who had previously been Chairman of Gawsworth Conservatives, was the Chairman, and Mr John Trueman, whose family still live in the parish, came on to the committee. Mr Trueman was the proud possessor of one of only two motor cars owned by Gawsworth inhabitants. It was an Overlander with a folding hood and just two half doors, which left an uncomfortable gap between the top of each door for the elements to enter. The headlights were mounted on both front mudguards, which stood out away from the bonnet.

On his way home from one meeting, John Trueman took Jas Hague along the main road back to his small farm (which later became a sand quarry and concrete mixing plant), and returning to the crossroads, he turned in at the top of Church Lane intending to drive through the village down Woodhouse End ('Woodarsend') towards Cow Brook lane. Unfortunately the car and the crossroads fingerpost had a confrontation. Later when he pulled onto the roadside down Woodhouse End Lane he discovered the Congleton finger lodged between his headlamp and the car bonnet and threw it over the hedge. The next day the village constable, investigating the incident, asked many questions of many villagers but despite the fact that there were only two cars in the village the crime remained unsolved. At the next Council meeting the minutes record how the members solemnly voted to replace the damaged fingerpost.

John Trueman was one of a group of farmers who often met up at The Royal Oak pub (now the Fool's Nook). They were fit hard men who had developed strength and stamina through hard graft. Twelve hour days were the norm and at harvest time they could work fifteen or sixteen hours, day after day, and it wasn't sitting on a tractor - it was muscle and pitch-fork harvesting. At other times they worked spades or muck-forks and carried two hundred weight sacks of grain on their backs. What developed was not bulging weight lifting type of muscles blown up by short bursts of power lifting in a gym. No these men had long sinewy supple muscles that gave them incredible stamina. It wasn't unusual for those young men in the prime of life to challenge each other. Often in my youth I watched, and even took part in, day long contests as farm workers tested out each others skill and durability whilst going about their everyday work in the fields. Every time the heavy built power-muscled men, while at first making the task look easy, faded as the day wore on.

Those contests were part of a day's work but after their working day was finished at the Royal Oak there were more contests. The challenge was to race up the field bank behind the pub carrying a barrel of beer on their shoulders. John Trueman took part in that but whether he took part in the following is doubtful. A very fit young farmworker, who had proved his strength in the barrel carrying, was challenged to walk home in the canal, which ran from the front of the pub to his home at Crow Holt Farm. I guess it is about 4 feet deep and about a half mile from pub to farm but it was also in winter when the water would be very cold. Nevertheless he did it. Alas a couple of days later he went down with pneumonia and died.

In the age of the pony and trap no one thought anything about taking a drink before picking up the reins and saying, "gee-up", mainly because the horse knew the way home. The tale is told of William Hockenull, the tenant at Park House Farm in Gawsworth, who followed his usual Friday routine by taking his wife to Macclesfield on market day. With the pony harnessed and hitched to the trap off they went, wife to do the weekly shopping and husband to mooch about the livestock market before settling his thirst in the pub.

On the way into town they had dodged in and out of road repairs taking place by the Rising Sun Hotel on the main Macclesfield to Congleton road. In those days stone for road repairs was tipped in small heaps along the road and then levelled by hand before the heavy steamroller finished the job off.

It was a warm day and the Hockenulls had been busy, the Missus round the shops and the Master in the cattle market and pub, so it was understandable if they felt a bit sleepy on the way home. When the pony and trap arrived back at Parkhouse farm yard the Hockenull's son said, "Eh Dad where's Mum?" Dad woke from his slumbers to exclaim, "Ee Lad I must have slattered her."

The Lad took the trap back and met Mum trudging homeward. Apparently with no one guiding him the pony hadn't bothered to trot round the heaps of road repair stone, so when the wheel bounced over one heap one of the occupants got a rude awakening while the other slept on. I wish I could have been in Park House farmyard when she finally caught up with her husband.

In my youth the stories of farmers who relied on their pony's homing instinct after indulging a little too much were numerous. One that I like came from my father-in-law. As a schoolboy he and some of his friends became aware that one local farmer was in the habits of hitching his pony and trap to a field gate by the side of the Trap Pub (now the Black Swan) in Lower Withington. At closing time he staggered out and released his steed, collapsed into the trap and relied on the pony to do the rest. While he was inside the lads unhitched the pony from the shafts and pushed them through the gate and hitched the pony back in again. When the farmer rolled out of the pub he kept asking the horse, "however did you get like this?"

One of my father's stories had no drink involved - in fact the man was a Methodist local preacher and local lads had planned their trick to catch him on his way home from taking evening service at the local chapel. They stuffed some old clothes with straw, used a turnip for the head, and with a carefully placed trilby laid the dummy on the side of the road. Of course there were no street lights or electric torches but even so the preacher saw the crude figure and stopped. Climbing down he walked over to the reclining shape and asked. "My dear man whatever have you been doing to get in into this state?" At least he didn't pass by on the other side.

There is another Methodist story worth telling. Modern TV plays and novels seem to typecast those Victorian christians as both pious and narrow-minded to the point of being cruel, but I believe it was seldom so. One local family was struggling to bring up eleven children on a small farm in Gawsworth. The father was a stalwart of the chapel - he had obviously done his best to keep the numbers up in the Sunday School. When one of the older girls 'got herself in trouble' there was no self righteous indignation or sending her away in shame. Dad just said, as many did, "we'll rear it as one of our own."

And so they had twelve. The youth supposedly involved got another girl 'in trouble' and then went off to fight in the Great War. He probably thought it was the safest place, and still he came through it unscathed.

Today's Gawsworth and North Rode

Perhaps the name Fitton is most associated with Gawsworth and its once large estate. Not only did the family own the estate for some 350 years, one member, Mary Fitton, was reputed to be the dark Lady of Shakespeare's sonnets. The last Fitton Baronet died fighting at the side of Prince Rupert in support of Charles I. After the King was beheaded in 1648 there seems to have been an uncertain time before the estate came into the hands of the Earls of Macclesfield in 1662.

A long drawn out dispute over the inheritance of the estates came to a head in 1712 when both contenders, Lord Mohun and the Duke of Hamilton, settled the argument at the point of a sword. Well two swords actually because both died of their wounds, which must have ended the argument without settling the disagreement. That went on for several years until the estate came into the possession of the Earls of Harrington, the Stanhopes, in 1727 and they held it until most of the estate was sold off in lots in 1920 and finally the Hall in 1937.

In woodland, close to the hall, one of the last of the court jesters is buried. I am not sure if in his day he was known as Lord Flame or Maggoty Johnson but the woodland has the latter name. Perhaps it should be Maggoty Johnson's canine shrine because Gawsworth's dog walkers take their pets to deposit their offerings haphazardly around the grave area on a daily basis.

In those olden days the Gawsworth estate stretched to Wilmslow in the North and into Staffordshire on the southern side but as previously stated the small estate of North Rode was not part of it. The Earls of Harrington had not lived in the Hall for some time. Some parts of it were unoccupied and the rest was in a divided tenancy; all of the property was allowed to decline. It remained in a neglected state until the Roper-Richards family took possession in more recent years.

Now the Hall and grounds stand in isolation of any estate. The present owners, Mr and Mrs Timothy Richards, have invested heavily to bring the Hall back to its former glory. To raise the funds for the expensive maintenance it is now open to the public and they also raise music and laughter in the gardens through the summer months to create more income. Perhaps Maggoty Johnson listens to the merriment with a professional smile on his ancient wrinkled face.

Although the estate had been reduced in size through the centuries it still must have been quite a sale when the Harrington Estate put most of the parish on the market in 1920. Each farm and cottage were sold individually. Some cottages were sold for as little as £10. Many of the farming tenants bought their own farm. Parkhouse Farm, which was originally 227 acres, was bought (either at the sale or soon after) by the County Council to be split into five smaller farms to help settle ex-soldiers after the First World War. It was a policy to create smaller farms this way, both to help ex-servicemen and to provide small starter farms generally. Several of Gawsworth's larger farms were divided up in this way. In 1929 my parents began their farming life on one such 42-acre County Council farm in Goostrey.

Surprisingly, around 1900, there were many larger farms than now, particularly in Gawsworth, and what is even more surprising is that on those large farms the field size was also equally large, in fact many were larger than they are today. Studying the old ordnance map of my immediate area there were several fields of around forty acres and at least one nearer to sixty acres, the size of the average Council Farm. So when the Council bought and divided a large farm into several, those large fields had to be subdivided if the small farmer was to be able to rotate his crops and graze his cows. There were other small farms with small fields, particularly in the village and its outskirts, but many of those have either been built on or used as playing fields.

The tenant of High Lane Farm, Richard Thornicroft, bought his at the auction for £1,800. Generations of his family had lived there as tenants since the 1830s. Richard was followed by his son Dick and more recently by his grandson Richard, who still farms there. Grandad Richard served on the Parish Council with John Trueman. Richard Thornicroft had a brother called Willsir. Apparently at the Christening when the Vicar asked, "And what do you name this child?" Mrs Thornicroft, showing her respect for the Vicar, said, "Will Sir." And Willsir he was for life. Most people though called him Will and his gravestone in the churchyard also just says Will.

There was another brother, Peter, who served part time in the Cheshire Yeomanry and was both a bit of a character and a crack shot. On one occasion, when representing his regiment in a shooting contest, as the day wore on he got more than a little tipsy. Although he got through to the final when it came to the shoot off the Colonel said, "Thornicroft you're too drunk to shoot." Peter said, "Just leave it to me, my Lord" - and he shot ten bull's-eyes out of ten to win.

Somewhere along the day's drinking beforehand he must have made an unusual bet because he not only rode home sitting backwards on his horse but he also had his trophy cup filled with beer at every pub between Chester and Gawsworth. The journey home took two weeks.

Peter had a reputation as being a very strong man. He proved it once by carrying an eighteen score pig's carcass from High Lane Farm to Gawsworth Hall. Although I think that would be its live weight, dressed out it would still be around 200lbs. To carry that weight for over half a mile was a considerable achievement. His son Hamo, who lived in Lowes Lane, was a builder mostly working on farms in the area. In France in the Great War he lay badly injured in a trench for four days without medical help. He later told his family the pain was so great that had he got hold of a gun he would have gladly shot himself. He lost one leg and one eye.

Hamo was a Thornicroft family name. The most famous Gawsworth Hamo was brought up at Big Tidnock where a branch of the Thornicroft family farmed for many years. He was the sculptor, Sir Hamo Thornicroft, whose famous stone carving of General Gordon of Khartoum is on the bank of the Thames. There is also another there of Boadicea and her chariot, which is most beautifully done. He gave a small statuette of King Alfred's mother to North Rode School but alas it was stolen many years ago when a twenty-first birthday party was held in the school room.

When researching these stories I learned that when the 20 railway arches were built in North Rode (elevation 113 feet, span 436 yards), although they were mainly of brick, a special rail line was laid to carry stone for the base from the Cloud. When they were completed in 1849 the small engine used was considered to be of no further use and was buried there. My 90 odd year old informant said she had been told about the engine by old Alec Davenport who lived at nearby Crossley Farm when they were constructed.

The two parishes saw a lot of disruption at this time because the Macclesfield Canal was opened in 1831, only eighteen years before the railway. To accommodate these major structures some country lanes were closed completely, and others diverted or cut off to leave the occasional farm or house isolated. The effect of 400 rough, hard drinking navvies moving into the area for three or four years would have been considerable.

The valley that later needed 20 arches to take the railway across, had also demanded considerable ingenuity to take a canal across. Built to connect South Manchester to the Potteries it was known as the Macclesfield Canal and by connecting it into the Peak Forest Canal it allowed, amongst other things, large quantities of lime to be transported out of the hills for use as fertiliser to sweeten the rich Cheshire grassland. Both lime and limestone were loaded on to canal barges at Buxworth Basin just south of Whaley Bridge. The barges could then sail along 23 miles of level water between Whaley Bridge and North Rode via Marple . In $1^1/4$ miles the canal then fell 118 feet., through 12 locks, and it had to be carried over the Dane on a steep earth embankment to a bridge about 50 feet. above the river.

The official records say that the Bosley Locks were designed by Thomas Telford, engineered by William Clowes and built by Messrs. Nowel and Sons, entirely of stone, with wooden gates. Each lock is 9 feet deep and with a stone built overflow pond and they are an incredible feat of 19th century engineering, well worth taking a stroll along them to see. The claim at the time was that they were "to exceed any in the kingdom".

Of course that amount of stone needed some serious quarrying on the Bosley Cloud which, local anecdotal stories claim, took the nose off the highest part of the hill and because there was an upward pillar of solid rock on that nose it also lowered its height (I've heard between 6 feet and 60 feet). The hard stone, cut into neat blocks weighing several hundredweights each, would need careful handling to get them down to the site. To achieve this (local tales handed down through five generations) a double rail line was built down the mountainside, with the weight of a load of stone going down one track hauling an empty truck up the other. I presume that the momentum took the truck all the way to the locks.

Although Thomas Telford was the consultant engineer, locals link James Brindley with the canal, which might seem strange because he died some 50 years before it was built. But the canal had been under discussion for some 70 years and the first 20 of those years were during the height of Brindley's career. Brindley was considered to be the most accomplished and versatile engineer of his day, in colliery drainage, water mills, milling machinery, water powered cranes and even an unusual steam engine with a wooden barrel (one I should think to stand well away from). His greatest achievement was the 375 miles of canals he surveyed, built or supervised; some of them finished by others after his death.

Brindley was reputed to have the ability to size up a problem and find the solution; sometimes retiring to bed for up to three days while he thought through a difficult problem and, although not illiterate as some have claimed, the solution would be only retained in his mind.

It is inconceivable that this difficult length of proposed canal was not originally surveyed by him - living in Leek it was right on his doorstep. He travelled on horseback to survey canals as far apart as Lancaster and Exeter, so Bosley would have been no more than a Sunday afternoon stroll.

From what I can gather the long delay was not so much the difficulty of building the canal but more that of persuading financiers to back the project and then convincing Parliament of its feasibility. There are records of Brindley riding to London on horseback to give evidence to Parliament of the feasibility of other canals. It would seem that Telford only visited the canal site at the planning stage and once more when it was nearly complete. I presume he also came for the opening ceremony.

It was the last major canal built in this country and the surprising thing was that by the time it was finished the Manchester to Liverpool Railway line was already in operation. The financial backers only put money into it because they believed that later it could be converted to a railway line, in fact a railway company bought the canal in 1834. Although the locks were spaced to provide a gradient suitable for a rail line I suspect it proved to have too many curves to convert, hence

the North Staffordshire Railway was built almost parallel to it, if a straight line can be parallel to a snaking one.

At that time Nathan Percival lived at Kiln Hill Farm in Bosley with a family of 10 daughters and one son. Some years before when his parents farmed there, his brother Sam went to Macclesfield one day and did not return. Although small schooners sailed inland as far as Northwich and Manchester it seems incredible that so far from the sea a press gang should take him - but they did, and there was no way he could let his family know. He was just not heard of again for many years. In those days methods of recruitment were a little more direct than today. Several years later when his mother was working in the kitchen she heard footsteps on the gravel path outside and, recognising them, she said immediately, "Sam's back".

Thomas Telford had recommended four separate reservoirs to supply the canal throughout the year but it was later found that just two were enough; one in Sutton and the larger one at Bosley, which was not finished until about three years after the canal was opened. The dam stands behind Kiln Hill Farm with the feeder stream from it running within a few yards of the house. It now makes a lovely feature in an attractive garden of what it is now Kiln Hall. Although the canal had to be closed in autumn 2003, through a shortage of water, the pleasure usage now far exceeds the commercial use in the middle of the 19th century.

By the time the canal was being built in the late 1820s, Nathan Percival's 10 daughters had become quite sophisticated young women whereas their brother was a bit rough and spent too much time at the pub. One night they took his clothes away and locked him in his room but he jumped out of the bedroom window and went to the pub in his underclothes. On another occasion the vicar was coming to have tea with the girls so they sent their disreputable brother to work down the fields out of the way. On his way home the vicar took the footpath across the fields and by chance met the lad who asked him, "How did you find the ladies, Vicar?"

The vicar replied. "Very well son, they are delightful."

The lad returned. "Ay, you have to live with the b-----s to know them."

Three of the daughters married civil engineers who I believe were involved in the construction of the canal, and one was Robert Brindley. I am not sure what his relationship to James was because records seem to show that James Brindley had just one illegitimate son, John Bennet, and two daughters from his second marriage. But James had three brothers, some of whom were involved in the canal business with him. Robert was probably a grandson of one of these.

Robert settled in this area, became a partner in the Bosley Works - or Mill as the locals call it (now Wood Treatment) - and lived in the large house standing above the works. Situated by the River Dane to make use of its water power the works was used for rolling and hammering copper, but later was converted into two cotton mills and a wood-turning establishment. In the 1850s it was occupied by three separate corn millers and a silk throwster. It was deemed important enough when the railway came to build a branch line down to it and there was even a Bosley railway station.

Rumour has it that the two partners of Robert Brindley got him drunk one night and tricked him into signing away his share of the works. He then took over his father-in-law's Kiln Hill Farm and farmed there until 1870. His great-grandson, Philip Buxton, who farmed the same farm, was an important figure in Cheshire farming circles, and took a hand in my life by persuading me to take office in the NFU. I wasn't too enthusiastic because we had two small children and a very large overdraft, but another elderly farmer, Clarence South, clinched the argument by tapping on my chest and saying, "Listen lad, if you don't do this, what will you do instead? You'll probably go down the fields and mend a fence or let a blocked drain off, and you will have forgotten about them in a couple of days. But if you do this, you'll remember it for the rest of your life."

It was a proud day for me to be elected chairman of the Macclesfield NFU and then Philip Buxton persuaded me to stand for the county chair. I lost the first contest against John Robinson, who made a considerable contribution to agriculture in Cheshire. Three years later I was nominated again and that time I won.

Back in the early 1900s, at the Gawsworth Parish Council, the farmers were demanding that the County Council took action to deal with the large flocks of sparrows and green linnets infesting the County. What my father's generation called a green linnet we now call a greenfinch. Today it is hard to understand just how numerous sparrows were then. As wheat crops were ripening they could descend in many thousands, and the action of perching on the ear of wheat shed much more grain than they took. The present Richard Thornicroft tells how he remembers his grandfather Richard firing both barrels of his twelve bore and killing thirty-two. They were skinned and made into a sparrow pie.

As a boy from the age of nine I was encouraged to shoot house-sparrows regardless of breeding season. Our farm's tall slate-roofed dutch barns (barns with a roof on corner posts without any side walls) were the nesting place for numerous swallows and house-martins. The larger, bullying, sparrows stole some of their nests and prevented them from occupying nearby nests. It was easy to tell which nest held sparrows because the entrance hole was enlarged and usually had an untidy bit of grass lining hanging out. I would shoot at returning sparrows and then shoot their nest down. It took a good number of airgun pellets to damage the mud built nest enough to evict Mrs Sparrow.

On the farm, shooting was a part of everyday life. For the working farmer there were not the organised pheasant shoots that we know of today. They were for the gentry. For the ordinary countryman rabbits were the sport of winter months. On dark windy nights long nets were used by a hardy few to good effect, but the real social sport was ferreting, when neighbours and relatives met together on each other's farms. Fitted in between morning and afternoon milking ferreting was a winter social event for the men and it raised a bit of much needed cash at the same time. It could only take place in mid winter because at other times there were nests of young rabbits to distract the ferrets from their work.

Throughout my youth those four or five winter days out with the ferrets were so enjoyable that I can still remember many incidents from them. We never used purse nets because it is impossible to lay them without making some noise and any disturbance above ground makes a rabbit suspicious enough to dodge around in the burrows rather than bolt. My father viewed purse nets as poacher's equipment, perhaps because it was a silent sport. The farmer on his own land could bang away at the freely bolting rabbits.

Going back to those financially hard days of the depression, just think if a sparrow was worth skinning, how much more was a rabbit worth? The poachers who threw the local bobby off the dam in North Rode were probably only after rabbits, but one successful night out with long nets could earn three or four men a week's wage each. The tenant farmers hated poachers, just as much as their landlord, because rabbits were a source of cash for them and they were their permitted sport.

There is an amusing story of how Willsir Thornicroft, when ferreting at Rode Green Farm, didn't see one rabbit bolt on his side of the hedge throughout the day. When they put the ferrets in the very last hole before returning home for milking, a rabbit bolted in front of Willsir. He put up the gun and then click-click; he had stood all day without a cartridge in his twelve bore.

The generations of Thornicrofts shared High Lane Farm House with generations of barn owls. Not literally - the barn owls, living in the attic, had their own private entrance high up on the gable end. In summer when the young had grown big enough to fly they became very noisy. There was much hissing, shushing and scolding as parents tried to persuade the young to take to the wing. The rest of the year the owls were reasonably quiet and unobtrusive neighbours, although the Thornicroft family had noticed a distinct bow in Grandfather Richard's bedroom ceiling for some while. Soon after he died in 1952, young Richard and his father Dick heard a house shaking thud and running upstairs discovered that, what had been Grandfather's bedroom ceiling, had fallen in. The bones and rubbish was three inches deep and it filled twenty-six corn sacks.

With the bedroom replastered Dick decided to use the master bedroom. What he hadn't realised was that the noise from above had previously been muffled by the accumulation of years of debris. It was now very audible through the thin ceiling. After a few nights of disturbed sleep because of the owls' talons scrabbling on the plasterboard above his head, Dick climbed into the loft and fixed a tight wire-netting floor about six inches above the plaster boards, but unfortunately as they bounced around on the tight wire-netting, the owls talons got hooked in it and would ping away as though someone was up there playing a guitar. Growing weary of their noisy neighbours the Thornicrofts reluctantly closed up the owl's entrance.

The owls moved to a nearby farm but still regularly hunted the Thornicrofts' barns. I can vouch for that because, when Celia and I were returning from a dinner dance late one evening we found an injured barn owl on the road just by High Lane Farm Drive. I stopped the car and Celia picked it up. She nursed it on the lap of her evening dress while I drove on in my penguin suit. Examining it in our farmhouse kitchen it lay relaxed in our hands but its big eyes watched our every move. Finally, deciding that it was injury free, Celia took it outside and placed it on the garden wall where it released a jet of the most evil smelling excrement you could ever meet. Fortunately it squirted between the evening dress and the penguin suit but had it been a few minutes earlier in the car!! On the wall the owl paused, swivelled his head round as only owls can do to take one last look at we strangely dressed people, and rose on silent wings into the night.

Living and working in the country has given me many opportunities to observe owls. For several years a pair of little owls nested in an old rabbit hole beneath an ancient thorn bush whose gnarled roots splayed out and clung precariously onto a dry hedge cop between two silage fields. I mowed the silage grass twenty-four hours ahead of the team of men who followed on to pick it up with forage harvester and trailers. One little owl, I presume it was the male, sat on a branch of an oak tree above the thorn bush to watch my every move with its most amazing articulating neck.

As my tractor passed by his eyes and little head turned as though riveted in line, if a branch blocked his vision he would duck or bob about and if that didn't work his neck seemed to extend like a periscope to keep those incredible eyes on my face. Each time I drove round the field to pass near his tree the same antics were repeated and they were repeated again the next day when the forage harvester roared past. After three or four years - perhaps one of the pair died or a rabbit had dug out the hole - they were no longer there and I missed them. But I still hear their noisy screeches from across the fields as the evening shadows lengthen.

Whereas mobile phones seem to be so intrusive when I am on the train or in town, in contrast the chorus of tewit-towoos that ring out around my home most nights as our tawny owls text message their extended family are very pleasant. They used to nest in a half-dead ash tree standing alongside our cow lane. The adults were very secretive, there was no bobbing about to give the nesting site away, but as the young owls grew nearer to maturity one sat in the entrance hole and again his large eyes followed every passing cow or tractor. When the winter storms disposed of that ash they moved into the wood behind my bungalow to nest in a semi-dead sycamore.

There are in fact two bungalows nestling side by side at the end of this fairly large block of woodland and the tawny owls seemed to find the mixture of shrubs, lawns and wild flowers surrounding them a productive hunting ground. The first year in the sycamore must have been successful for food because we were sure that there was at least three young (I say 'we' because my neighbour Phillip is equally interested). Once the young had flown the nest, most evenings they came to sit around in the oaks along the wood edge calling to mum for food. I learnt to imitate the owlets' 'mum-come-feed-me' call well enough to entice them into the oak tree behind my garage, where one occasionally came within an arms length.

One dark night I was leaning against the garage wall trying to call my feathered neighbours, and although one replied from further along the wood edge, my repeated calls brought him no nearer. This owl conversation had gone on for some twenty minutes before I realised that the answering owl was Phillip trying to do the same as me.

The following year Phillip climbed up to the nest before the young flew. There was just one fat fluffy baby owl sitting among a nest strewn with blackbird feathers. We presumed that because of a very wet winter the water table had risen so high that many of the wood mice (their normal diet) had drowned during winter hibernation. Hence the tawny's diet of blackbirds, which alas had not been sufficient to save the young one's weaker siblings from making the ultimate sacrifice.

The dead sycamore came to grief in the winter storms so Phillip placed a nesting box high in a larch. Although it has been used I have not seen a brood since - or perhaps it is just that they have stayed clear of my garden.

Perhaps you have a romantic view of how the countryside was in those olden days. Yet it is still basically the same today. Yes I know there are large fast moving tractors and massive combine harvesters, but saw mills, blacksmiths and steam engines weren't all that quiet you know. Then again many local people are still there, many of them, as we saw from Gawsworth's records, with roots in their parish that go back generations. Of course many outsiders are buying up property and settling into country life, while many more visit just for a day or a weekend. To many of them the countryside is no more than a giant playground to tramp across in brightly coloured jackets or fly over in microlites. It is very hard on such short visits to relate to everyday country life around them.

Macclesfield Borough Council decided for a millennium project to make a photographic record of local people going about their everyday lives in the year 2000. About halfway through the year Celia, my wife, was asked to cover the seven parishes round our home stretching from Bosley to Lower Withington; her brief was to make a photographic record of country people at work and play.

The year was over before she realised that field sports had been missed. So early in 2001 in one hectic but enjoyable week I acted as driver while Celia followed foxhounds, beagle hounds and joined a shooting party. Her final invitation was to join a couple of friends for a days ferreting but with a skittering of snow and a cold east wind I nobly said, "You don't really need me today do you?"

Just as cricketers wear white (except when they wear pyjamas), and you can usually recognise someone on the way to a golf club, so each of the traditional country sports has developed its own dress code. Celia had some super photos and I have tried to capture the same in words with a mixture of country humour and pride. Pride to be a part of a way of life that sadly is fast being eroded.

'I knows me place'

Each countryman must have his place,
In this we're different from the urban race.
Others must know where each man should stand,
Among the rustics, be they humble or grand.

The country gentleman's plus four tweeds,
Say loud and clear that he has few needs.
With his Range Rover parked and his lab by his feet,
On the shooting field he can be seen at his peak.
The beaters are there with their old boiler suits,
Tucked into their mud-smeared wellington boots.
Over, my Lord, no I think you misheard,
That shortsighted one just shot a running bird.

The beagle hounds seem to have followers clear,
Of any and every other country peer.
With smart green jackets and clean white britches,
They're hardly dressed for jumping wide ditches.
With accents that give vent to an upper class,
They chase after hounds through the long wet grass.

The Foxhunter though is in a different sphere,
A redcoat, britches and a horse, oh so dear.
With his toes turned out and his nose turned up,
He starts his day with a stirrup cup.
Then risking his life at considerable cost,
He chases a rogue fox till it's killed or it's lost.

The horses whinny, the loud hound dogs bay,
But the sly old fox may still have the last say.
From the goose on the pond, to the hen in the garden,
Even the gambolling lamb, he'll give none a pardon.

The humble yokel knows his place so lowly,
With freezing toes waits his prey more slowly.
His ferrets are down and he's waited long,
For the burst of a rabbit in his purse net strong.
But his old army coat keeps the foul weather out,
Till he's back in the pub with a glass of brown stout.

Dressed for our parts like cricketers in whites,
Though none so ridiculous as a cyclist's tights,
We make fun of each other yet respect each his lot,
Then we all pull together through life's diverse plot.

Now you urban yuppies in your bright coloured clad,
Have not yet grasped what has got us all mad.
In our old dull brown jackets we still live by a code,
Which for hundreds of years has put food on the road.
It's not for the taking, it's a tough way of life,
So just leave us to live it without all this strife.

If that hasn't made you smile and reflect, the following three stories I hope
will. They intend to capture the occasional visitor's experiences; the first two
are short while the third takes you on a much longer emotional journey
between the City of London and the Peak District.

This Could be Heaven

I was speeding. Yes I admit it. The road was wet, the night was dark and I wanted to get a couple of hours sleep before an early turnout to fish as the sun rose. It wasn't often that I could get away from the city for a couple of days but I had and I was going to make the most of it. So, yes I was travelling too fast when that cow walked out of a dark gateway. Not that I remember much after that; just the horror of knowing I wasn't going to stop, then the splintering glass.... and then those white coats round my bed.

Mind you I'm not sure that it was a bed, perhaps it was only a hospital trolley with people bustling around me. I heard one say, "I think he's going!" Then another said. "No he's still here - but I think he will go."

Perhaps they were planning to send me home, I don't really remember much. Anyway it's all best forgotten now because I am here at last! No, I mean I'm really here! Here beside my favourite water. Oh I know it's only a small river but that's what I like and what's more the sun's shining and the water is just right.

An old man came to me as soon as I got here, and offered to act as my gillie. He seems a strange, even an odd sort of character with not much to say; just, "I'll be your gillie, Boss." Then he pointed out which fly he recommended. Now he's pointing to where a large brown trout is rising.

So here goes then; one cast to straighten out my line; now the next cast should drop the fly right on the fish. Bang, he's on! Wow what a lively fish, splashing, fighting and leaping from one side of the stream to the other.

Now he's off down stream.... gosh he has some power, line's streaming off my reel. I think I've turned him, yes he's coming back but he's fighting all the way. What a fighter. What a tussle, but at last he's coming into the net. Gosh he must be all of three pounds.

Let me get him out of the net to take a better look. Hang on, the gillie's pointing to another fish. Well that is incredible, would you believe it, there is another fish rising in just the same place.

"Alright, let's not be impatient. I'll put a line out to it in a moment." I tell him slightly irritated at not being able to look at the fish I've caught.

And so I cast again. Would you believe it, I've hooked this one too. What's more it looks much the same size as the first one. And it fights just like the first one. Wow what a lively fish, splashing, fighting and leaping from one side of the stream to the other. He's off down stream again.... gosh what power, the line's streaming off my reel. I've turned him, he comes back towards me but he's fighting all the way. What excitement. He's coming towards the net; and all of three pounds again.

It really was a struggle but at last he's in the net. Now I'm going to have a proper look at both of them. They are two beautiful fish, identical in size with the same brightly spotted bodies. You know, I could just sit here and admire them for an hour.

Hang on, the old gillie's pointing a gnarled finger to another fish, and it's rising in just the same spot! "Look!" I tell him, growing impatient. "This brook could be Heaven if you would just leave me alone to enjoy it!"

The old gillie turned and this time stabbed his gnarled finger at me. "Let's get one thing straight Boss; this isn't Heaven - this is Hell! So pick up that rod and keep fishing!"

The First Time

Rosemary Dunge-Lovatt stared up at the sky one day and swore. She was lying on her back behind a haystack and feeling rather sore.

Noticing that overhead the moon was canted on its side, she marvelled. Not so much because it was leaning sideways or even because it was overhead - it was just that she had never noticed it in the mid-morning gray light of winter before.

Nearer to her, Jeremy's face seemed so close, as his eyes gazed into hers. Slowly her breathing steadied down and her chest no longer felt that it would burst.

She swore again at him, at what he had persuaded her to do, and at the damp hard ground. "Why did I let you talk me into this?"

"You know that you've been wanting to do it for a long time. Anyway it was either today or wait for another month until we could be together again."

"Yes - but it should be better than this!" Miss Dunge-Lovatt complained as she sat up and began to brush the bits off her clothes.

Trying to console her, Jeremy, holding out his hand to help her up, said, "It's often like this the first time, but I think we should try again, it will be better next time?"

"Yes..... alright!" She whispered, shakily holding onto his hand while he brushed the bits off her back.

"Yes, alright! It has to be now though, before I change my mind.....   But if that stupid horse throws me off like that again, it will be the last time I go out hunting with you."

Author's note:
This story is fictitious and does not refer to any known person or place

City Shepherd

Chapter 1

L ast year they had spent a weekend walking in the limestone area of the Peak District National Park. It was called the White Peak and it contrasted dramatically to their location this weekend. Trev and his two friends were on the Cheshire side of the Park this time, amongst the dark sombre gritstone hills above Macclesfield, and they had come with the intention to just walk, eat and sleep.

On the first afternoon they did a short walk, and now on the second day they started out early to walk across the moors above the Clumber valley. They had not gone more than a mile when Trev saw a sheep that he thought must be trying to lamb. Not that he knew much about sheep but when he was a teenager his pet dog had given birth to a litter of pups so he recognised the signs, head thrown back, lips curled up and the obvious straining in the prostrate body. Anyway his grandfather had been a farmer, not that he remembered much about that because the old man had died when he was only eight, nearly twenty years ago. But there were times when he imagined that he would recall mental pictures of cows or haymaking or some other event that must have taken place when he had visited the farm with his parents. The trouble was he was never sure if it was a real memory or just what his mind conjured up from something he had read or seen on TV.

Trev felt sure there was a problem with this sheep but when he tried to explain it to his friends they wanted a clearer explanation and Trev couldn't give one. "Look we are here for a break, we have just three days, so let's make the most of them. Anyway the farmer'll be around somewhere."

When Trev pointed to the ewe and said "but...." They both ignored him and walked on. Torn, between two desires, Trev slipped his rucksack off his back and sat down uncertainly on a low rocky outcrop. After watching the ewe for nearly a half an hour he was convinced she was in trouble. Some other hikers came by but when he tried to ask their advice, they just shrugged their shoulders, muttered something about farmers knowing their own business, and went on their way.

There had been a farm homestead nestling among two or three neatly walled and green fields behind the hill, perhaps a half-mile from where they had parked earlier that morning. Noticing a little path leading off in that direction, Trev set out towards where he thought the farm lay. What had looked an easy downhill walk proved to be a lot of little ups as well as downs. When he finally knocked on the farmhouse door he was quite out of breath, and although usually precise and exact in his nature, Trev found himself stumbling over his words as between deep breaths he tried to explain something about a sheep trying to lamb.

Studying him carefully for a moment, the old farmer said. "Alright lad, come in and tell me about it while I finish my breakfast."

When he breathlessly repeated what he had seen the old man replied. "Aye well it happens sometimes. These old ewes hide from th' dogs at roundup, then they're out on th' moor on their own when lambing time comes."

He spread homemade jam liberally across a piece of toast while his wife poured out a beaker of tea for Trev. It was only a matter of minutes before the farmer had swallowed his own tea and rose to reach down his coat from by the hot stove. "Well lad, we'd better go take a look then."

Gulping down the last of his hot tea, Trev jumped to his feet to follow. The old farmer set off at a deceptively casual yet long striding pace. Trev was soon struggling on the up bits - and going back there were a lot more ups than downs. There wasn't much conversation.

A rough coated black and white dog, which had joined them as they left the house without a word or a whistle from its boss, now ranged ahead. The farmer said little as the dog sniffed with curiosity at every rock and tree stump.

Soon a blue fatigue haze seemed to be hovering in front of Trev's eyes. At last to his relief they reached the place where he had seen the ewe, which had moved a little but they soon found it. When they walked closer it set off at a gallop but the dog was in front in a flash. Then while the ewe was stamping her feet and trying to get past the dog the farmer just walked up and caught hold of her.

While Trev was still gasping for breath the old farmer had rolled her over and felt under her tail. "Well here you are lad, you've done all th'hard work, now do you not want to finish it off an help it out?"

And so Trev lambed his first ewe. It was easy really, just a big single tup lamb with a head a bit to big. When he pulled on its protruding front legs it slid out into the world and gasped its first breath. But Trev was hooked.

Sitting companionably together on the rocky outcrop, the contrast in the two was dramatic; one dressed in a bright red, ultra expensive, breathable walking coat; the other in a torn and scruffy waxed jacket. Even their boots contrasted sharply - smart suede against unpolished strong leather. Trev explained why he was on his own and how his two companions would now probably be making their way back to the hotel in their flash sports car. As they talked the lamb managed to get his back feet under him but try as he might, he seemed unable to straighten his front legs. When the ewe turned sideways on to the lamb, to Trev's amusement, he was soon sucking away while still on his knees.

"He'll clog it now," said the farmer, getting up from the stone and turning towards the farm. Seeing how fascinated Trev was with the lamb, he paused. "Look lad if you are interested you could come back with me for a while - there's another four hundred ewes back near th'farm."

They took the walk a little more leisurely this time, which allowed them to get introduced properly and for Trev to ask a few questions. It seemed it was the lambing season and to give Trev an idea what that meant Jim lead him to a rocky ridge where they looked over into a small sheltered valley, seemingly full of sheep.

"We lamb in this sheltered little valley but move them out onto th' in-bye pastures as soon as the lambs are strong enough. Mind you singles like that one we've just left can go straight out."

Trev studied the layout. Only about 100 metres wide with a smaller narrow ridge along the far side, there were three dividing walls creating three small fields and, below where they were standing, a wall ran across the end of all three small fields. He could see that whoever had built it had meandered the wall to make use of where the natural solid rock could form the boundary, while elsewhere the wall stood a good four feet tall. Dotted about among the ewes and lambs, other boulders jutted up out of the turf. On the far side, a low up-thrust of rocks formed a natural shelter barrier along the top field, and a tall stonewall did the same along the other two fields. Between that and a distant hill he presumed there must lay a valley. Trev thought he ought to say something, "Do you call these in-bye fields, then?"

"No, there's too many rocks up here. In-bye land is down yon, round th' farm buildings. Grandad cleared a couple of fields there when me Dad were a lad so he could plough and make hay on 'em. That's where I put these ewes once they've lambed and when I'm sure th' lambs are strong enough to clog it."

"But there are a lot of lambs still in here aren't there?"

"Aye lad there is. Me and th' dog keep popping 'em through the gates on th' far side but there's above a hundred ewes in here still to lamb, so we don't chase em round; just dodge ewes and lambs out when we can."

To Trev's inexperienced eyes there seemed to be a confusion of bleating ewes calling to errant and equally noisy lambs. Reading his thoughts Jim said, "Most of 'em know what they're doing. There's just a few like the one we've just lambed that need help, and those with twins want watching."

Again he read Trev's mind. "One lamb gets away from th' ewe while she's straining with th' second one; its worse at th' start when th' fields are fuller, or if we get a bit of snow. Come on, let's go down and check them."

And so Trev got another lesson in sheep husbandry. There was one ewe trying to lamb hidden behind the wall. Jim soon caught it with the dog's help, but when they pulled it out the lamb was dead. Seeing Trev's downcast face Jim said, "Eh lad you can't win em all. We'll look round the others, then I'll soon put a lamb on this ewe."

Pointing to a pair of twin lambs born that morning, one was on its feet, little tail wagging furiously as it suckled hungrily, while the other was trying to balance on unsteady legs. Jim said, "It has suckled, look you can see its stomach's full. It was this pair that made me late for breakfast; they were both trying to come out at th' same time."

In the far corner of the field there was a small stonewalled pen with a sheet of corrugated iron weighted down by several rocks, forming a crude roof as a shelter for the ewe inside. Jim explained, "She's got two lambs but hasn't got enough milk for them both so one lamb' s weakly. It'll soon rally when we put it on that other ewe; here you carry it."

Unsure what was happening, Trev tucked the small lamb under his arm and followed Jim across the field to where the ewe was still forlornly licking the still form of her new born lamb. Dropping onto one knee, with the ewe bleating and barging round in consternation, Jim slipped a sharp knife from a sheath and expertly slit the skin down the dead lambs belly then down each leg. With movements too quick for Trev to follow the woolly skin was tugged free and throwing the carcass well away, Jim said, "Slip your lambs back legs in here."

Once each hind leg had gone in through a slit in the thigh skin of the dead lamb, Jim deftly repeated the move with the two front legs. Muffled in his woolly topcoat, the little lamb looked a strange ungainly picture, but not to the mourning ewe. She rushed forward to smell and lick and smell again. With the leg skin of the dead lamb dangling over his own ungainly legs, in less than a minute the underfed lamb was guzzling at a much fuller milk bar.

"He'll clog it now," was all the old farmer said.

They dropped the carcass into a large plastic drum near to a small hut in the corner of the middle field, which Trev hadn't noticed until Jim led him to it. In the hut, along one side, the rear seat from an old bus acted as either a bed or seat. A small table, two chairs and a calor gas heater made up the rest of the furniture. It was a long time since breakfast and Trev began to think about the packed lunch and flask in his rucksack. When he offered to share it Jim said, "Nay lad, I'm off home for a bite. Missus'll come round in a bit while I catch an hours sleep, then I'll be out again before tea. But you sit yourself down in th' warmth and enjoy your baggin."

Sitting at the table underneath the one window Trev found he had a good view down the narrow middle field. He watched one ewe pottering around seemingly restless but never leaving the same place by the wall. "Her's uneasy, her'll lamb soon," he seemed to hear his grandfather say in the depths of his mind. Yes that was just what his grandfather would have said. He had been having memory flashes like this all morning. Little things about the baby lambs and the ewes, nothing much, it was just as though he knew instinctively where to walk among them and how to hold that small lamb. Now it all seemed to come back in a flash. He remembered sitting on a bale of straw next to his Grandad - because his flock of lowland sheep lambed in January they were under the dutch barn - when his Grandad said, in his broad Shropshire dialect, " Watch that one Trev, her's uneasy, her'll lamb soon."

More memories flooded back. It was the end of the Christmas holidays, he was due back at school in the New Year and Grandad's sheep had just started to lamb. He was smiling to himself about how he had tried to stay up with his Granddad until he became so sleepy that he had to be carried upstairs to bed.

Trev's journey down memory lane was interrupted when the shed door rattled open and a tall slim woman stepped through. "Hello, you must be Trev! I'm Marion. Jim said he thought you would still be here; he says you seem interested in these sheep of ours."

His chair clattered over as he jumped to his feet. "Yes I suppose I am. I'm surprised how much I am."

He was also surprised at Marion's youthful looks and clear skin. Was it because she was much younger than Jim or was it just that his weathered face and bowed shoulders reflected toil rather than years? Again Marion broke into his thoughts, "Is there anything happening out there?"

"That one's uneasy, I think she will lamb soon." Following his pointing finger with her eyes Marion replied, "I think you are holding out on us, you've done this before."

Trev told her of his few incomplete memories as they walked round the three fields. It was only when Marion called her dog that Trev realized it wasn't actually Jim's dog Gyp. Marion said. "Old Gyp won't work for me. He lets me feed him and fasten him up but after that he just ignores me. These feminist campaigners want to try working old Gyp, he reckons nothing to women. My Floss can't hold a ewe like Gyp can, but we manage."

Trev knew that Marion didn't mean literally that the dog held the ewe - but held it by the power of its eye. It was soon demonstrated when one ewe, needing help to lamb, managed to dodge both Floss and Marion before Trev brought the sheep down with a rugby tackle.

It was soon time to walk back towards the car. Trev could have walked down the farm drive and along the lane but he wanted to retrace his morning's walk across the footpath. Jutting boulders were casting long shadows across the moor when he paused to look for his ewe and lamb. It took a few minutes to find them sheltering in a peat hag. He laughed at the thought that this morning he had no idea what a peat hag was. Now, thanks to Jim, he knew the name for a sharp depression where the peat had been eroded.

Trev got a lot of ribbing from his two companions over the evening meal when he explained a little of his adventure. They split their sides with 'Good Life' and 'back to your roots' quips, and he joined in the laughter. The next morning he wanted only to return to the sheep. but he felt compelled to walk with them. They had planned a short walk for it was Monday morning and they had planned to motor home after lunch. Trev walked with them, and joined them for a bar snack but when the other two slid down into the sports car's bucket seats, Trev waved them off and turned his own car back towards the farm.

He arrived just as Marion started out on the afternoon shift and Trev fell instep beside her. There were no ewes to lamb or dead lambs to skin today, just a pleasant hour looking round the sheep and chatting to Marion. Back at the farmhouse he was washing down a large slab of fruitcake with a beaker of tea when Jim came down the stairs. He found the couple very easy company, there was no desperate urgency about their actions nor did there seem to be any tension between them. Jim tucked into some cake before setting off to look round the lambing fields again before dark.

Trev climbed into his car and set off back towards London. He left with a firm invitation from to come back later in the year and stay with them for a week.

Chapter 2

Planning holidays was not easy because Trev had a girlfriend. Not that any of his colleagues at the merchant bank knew about Naomi. They knew her as a very attractive but cool executive working on a floor - and a company level - above Trev. The bank was very strict about office romances; any hint of such between them would bring instant dismissal - and Trev thought that with her seniority and the present fear of sex discrimination it was more likely that he would be the sacrificial lamb.

Naomi took great care over their secret, to the extent that even mobile phone calls were only made in emergency. So it was just text messages and a twice-weekly date. She never allowed him to visit her in her flat but kept a key to his, which was used most Wednesdays and Sundays when Naomi slipped into a fetching tracksuit and seemingly left her own flat to take exercise. The following morning she jogged back home again to quickly change before getting off to the office. What happened in between was satisfying enough for both of them to have continued their unusual arrangement since they met at the office Christmas party some year and a half before.

They also managed the occasional weekend away and a fortnight of sun and sand on some remote island. Even so Naomi was so paranoid about secrecy that it put a damper on it. The weekends that Trev visited his separated parents, both now remarried, he would return home mid-Sunday evening to find a romantic candlelight dinner waiting. Sometimes even that was missed out and they went straight to the real business. Trev had learned to keep his fridge well stocked for midnight snacks.

The large private bank had many clients who traded across the world. To finance the day-to-day business the bank had to carry staggering sums of foreign currency; many larger customers notified the bank of their foreign currency requirements weeks ahead of transactions. Trev dealt in currency; sitting in front of flickering monitors clinching deals to buy or sell millions at the blink of an eyelid and the flick of a finger. When he bought was up to him, as long as the currency was there when it was needed. He might deal with a month to spare or have a nail-biting time waiting until the very last minute. In the office by 6.30 to catch up on the world money markets and after a hot bacon butty at around 8.15, Trev lived on adrenalin throughout his working day. Although there were five others in his department, each dealt in different currencies and each answered individually for their decisions. But he was good at his job, and the bank recognised just how good when they dished out a seven-figure New Year bonus.

After her divorce his mother had returned to her roots, as she put it, to find peace of mind. She had renewed a teenage romance and was now married to the village butcher, Bob. On the other hand, his father, always a city man, was now married to a beautiful and sophisticated city girl, little older than Trev - and although they made him welcome when he called, it was to his stepfather's modest three bed-roomed house in Shropshire that he usually escaped to about once a month.

It was on one such weekend when his stepfather was slicing up the Sunday roast that the talk turned to the price of lamb. Trev's mum seemed a little surprised at his sudden interest in food but then he explained about his weekend in Cheshire. His butcher stepfather took up the cue and informed him at length about the decline in farming profits. Trev headed back towards London with four choice lamb chops to the usual Sunday night assignation with his dusky skinned maiden. From experience he knew that the long night would be more enjoyable if it began with a simple meal - and what better than some delicious red meat.

Trev and Naomi had enjoyed a fortnight of winter sun in early spring, and she had decided that for her second holiday she would pay a visit to her paternal grandmother in Nigeria again. Although Trev had never met her parents he was well aware of how proud Naomi was of them; of how they had overcome any prejudice there had been over their mixed marriage and of how her father supported his relatives out in Nigeria. Naomi visited her grandmother most years - which left Trev free to decide again where and when to take his summer holiday.

Trev's office view was one of endless multi-story buildings interwoven with honking motor cars crawling along impatiently. The more he looked, the more he longed for the gritstone hills of Cheshire again. So he stopped and typed the letter to Cheshire to ask if he could stay and if so when might he be most useful. The hearty welcome from Jim and Marion returned. "Come for the second week in September to help with the gather. There's always plenty on then."

There were too many loose rocks and boulders on Jim's moor for him to safely use a quad bike. Trev again tried to match the easy but ground covering farmer's stride. Over a pre-daybreak cold breakfast Jim had explained that they had to gather in the cool of the morning or the dogs would over-heat, particularly Gyp because of his rougher coat. Although it was the younger bitch, Gem, who did the biggest out-run. She was what Jim called 'an upright runner' - a dog that neither crouched nor commanded sheep by eye control but kept on the move and was ideal for gathering out on the moor. And being short coated she should stay reasonably cool through the morning's work.

As the sun broke above the rocky hills to the east of the moor a red glow dazzled them and highlighted the rocks and boulders strewn around. Pausing to look back, the view was breathtaking, but Trev was almost too breathless to say, "I never see views like this on a Monday morning."

Acknowledging briefly the beauty of the scene, Jim said, "Aye but it'll rain before th' days far gone so let's push on."

Trev watched Jim and his two dogs. He was fascinated at how the older Gyp calmly watched Jim send the young one out far across the moor. Marion had taken a shorter path onto the other side of the moor opposite, and pointing into the far distance Jim said. "Gem should meet Floss beyond that crag then with luck they'll both turn back and work inwards."

Distant white shapes of recently shorn sheep began to move towards them. At first the movement was broken by long pauses, when the ewes looked back trying to decide if the round up was for real or not. Eventually they must have decided it was because they came on skipping friskily over rocks and dodging around boulders. Then individual groups of sheep joined others as they came nearer until at times they looked like one white stream running between the rocky outcrops.

It was well over an hour since Gem had gone out and Gyp was fretting to join the action, so when Jim saw about ten ewes and lambs trying to dodge back along the perimeter wall he just pointed and Gyp was off. When all the sheep had passed by in the direction of the farm Jim called the dogs across to where a spring welled out from beneath a rocky outcrop. Gem just flopped down in the icy cold water, and even Floss came across to splash and lap thirstily. It took another hour to push the sheep down into the first of the lambing fields with Gyp now doing the bulk of the work.

Marion had left a casserole in the Rayburn to simmer gently through the morning. It was at midday that they, like most farmers, took their main meal. Never having tasted anything so delicious before Trev raised a questioning eyebrow and said, "Venison?"

"Aye lad," Jim grinned, "It was a yearling hind that got caught up in our boundary fence and broke a leg. The neighbour and me.... well we kind of rescued it from the wire and put it in the deep freeze."

The rain came on heavy before they had finished, delaying till next day the heavy work of worming and sorting. Jim explained that he would wean the wether lambs (castrated tups) now. The few that were ready for the butcher they would keep separate but the rest would be kept on the in-bye fields to be sold at different local store sheep sales. The ewe lambs were to go back onto the moor with their mothers until October when they would also be weaned and sent off to a lowland farm to live on a richer grass through the winter months. He explained that the sparse heather was all right to rear them on but it wouldn't grow the ewe lambs or fatten the wether lambs good enough for the meat trade.

It took two days to separate wether lambs from the ewes, sort fat from thin then give a worming drench to those lambs not ready for slaughter and drive them into the small lambing fields until they got over the trauma of losing their mums. At the end of the second day Trev was feeling the effects. So he was relieved when Jim decided to leave dipping the lambs until Friday and take the thirty fat ones to Chelford's Thursday fatstock market.

The bustle of the market as dozens of farmers in four wheel drives skilfully manoeuvred loaded cattle and sheep trailers backwards to the unloading ramps fascinated Trev. To him the thirty fat lambs looked alike as peas in a pod but Jim pointed out the subtle differences as he sorted them into five matching lots and put each six-lamb lot in different pens. There was time for a cup of tea in the canteen before a loudspeaker announced the sale. On a catwalk above the pens the auctioneer moved from pen to pen with a quick eye and a poised stick. "Jim's lambs here. Straight from the hill this morning; where are you going to start me?" The stick was raised to point at various bidders but the gabble was too quick for Trev to follow, and suddenly the stick struck the catwalk as the auctioneer announced the buyers name and moved on to Jim's next pen.

Friday had been set aside for dipping the rest of the wether lambs. That it was a miserable wet day didn't deter Jim who said, "Up here, if you stopped work because of rain you'd do nothing." Fortunately Trev had brought a good waterproof suit, which he donned to trudge off with Jim to bring in one bunch of lambs. There was no romantic view across the moor, just a trudge out to the lambing fields and a lot of arm-waving and shouting as about 130 lambs were crowded into the pre-dipping pen. The funnel shaped pen led to the below ground dip where at one end a smooth stone flag lay alongside, at a forty degree angle.

Jim caught a lamb and placed it in the corner just beyond that flagstone and said, "Right then" to Trev who was standing with the other lambs. He hadn't a clue what should happen next but Marion's reassuring voice from behind said. "It's all right, Trev, just wait while Jim gets in place and then let them go."

By that time Jim was standing alongside the long sheep dip holding a crazy looking crook. Dressed in heavy waterproofs Marion now demonstrated the art of sheep dipping. As the lamb beyond the stone bleated, others, trying to join it, jumped onto the sloping flagstone and slipped in with a splash. As the lambs swam past Jim he pushed each lambs head under and guided them out at the far end where they stood bedraggled and forlorn in a draining pen with the excess liquid pouring from their fleece, back into the dip. When enough lambs had gone through to fill that pen Marion stopped the others until Jim opened the gate into the second draining pen. When that one was full the first pen was let go.

The dipping went on through the morning but not without effort because the trick flagstone only worked if they kept crowding the rest of the lambs tight up to it. Occasionally a lamb, twigging the danger of the sloping stone, refused to jump onto it, and then they had to lift it on and into the dip. Trev's fancy waterproofs soon reeked of the evil smelling sheep dip, which the rain dribbling off his nose and down his neck failed to disperse.

Was he thankful that the resourceful Marion had left another casserole to gurgle away while she was with the sheep - and Trev didn't let the smell of sheep-dip deter him. After the delicious meal and resting for an hour, they all slid into waterproofs and repeated the process with another group of lambs. That night Trev slept heavier than he could remember doing for years.

Saturday was a rest day, which meant that Jim had time to walk his moor to check through the ewes and ewe lambs. Of course Trev went along with him. He was stiff but the day turned warm and the scenery was covered with an unusual softness, and was deep with early autumnal tinges. He felt more relaxed and at peace with the world than he had for a long while.

It was showery again on Sunday morning so when Jim and Marion drove off to morning service Trev decided against a walk in the rain; instead he would drive over to Buxton. Driving the length of the valley to join the Congleton to Buxton road he had only gone a short distance along the main road when he saw an advert for farmhouse ice cream - he just had to stop. The rain stopped and he was surprised to find that behind the farm shop cum café was an outdoor dining area with a superb view back along the clough. The ice cream was delicious and as there was a promise of baked potatoes and hot apple pie on the meal board, he changed his direction into North Staffordshire; taking a short scenic route that would bring him back to the café for midday.

On Monday morning Trev learned what many farmers think about hikers when they went to look round the wether lambs. Where the footpath crossed the in-bye fields there was a stone stile built into the wall, now on either side of it the top third of the dry stonewall had been pushed off. The damage was more than someone just climbing carelessly and knocking an odd stone of the top. Seeing the wall and that the carefully sorted lambs were now mixed together again, Jim let out something about 'bagrats'. It was a few minutes before Trev realised just what was meant by the expression, and two days before he really understood Jim's anger. What an irresponsible walker -or to use Jim's expression a 'stupid b----- bagrat' had knocked down in two minutes, took them two days and an aching back to rebuild.

"If we've got to get those lambs in to re-sort them we may as well take a bunch to the store sale on Saturday." said Jim over breakfast.

Trev had planned to travel back to London that day because he had his usual date planned for Sunday night and he needed a little time to shop for the coming week. Still the chance to visit an autumn sheep fair was not to be refused. Jim explained that he could only fatten about half of his wether lambs on his more lush in-bye fields so some lambs were sold at the autumn fairs, when lowland farmers bought hill lambs to finish them on their richer grass through the winter months.

The sale ring was just a large tent in the middle of a field. Around it hundreds of hurdle pens had been erected in a complex arrangement so that each pen opened onto an alleyway and each alleyway led to the sale ring. Two or three country children drove each pen of lambs into the ring, waited while they were sold, then drove them down a different alley back to the pen. The auctioneer stood on a rickety looking rostrum opposite to the ring gates and on the other two sides of the ring straw bales were built up to form three tiers of seating. Smartly dressed lowland farmers mixed around the ring with the rugged-faces of local hill farmers. Jim introduced him to numerous friends and relatives - Trev was surprised how many of the hill farmers were related and how their lives were so interwoven.

When Jim's lambs came into the ring he went in with them to help drive them round so that everyone could get a good view. From the antics of the auctioneer it would seem that the bidding was brisk and within a couple of minutes Jim was handing over a £5 note for luck money to a tall dignified man in a tweed suit.

They left the sale ring to eat a beef bap, sitting on a bale of straw in the improvised canteen. Trev sat there listening to the drone of sheep talk around him while Jim queued to draw his money. A little later, driving out of the now very rutted field, Jim reflected on the day. "That's my harvest, then, lad. My total sheep sales take place in less than two months. Good trade or bad they have to go, and that's it for the year."

Chapter 3

A fortnight away from Naomi meant that their urgency was too great to relax over a Sunday evening meal. It was a midnight feast of cheese, biscuits and an apple.

Next morning back in his office the emails and flickering monitors all spewed out their graphs, trends and predictions at an alarming rate. Trev found it hard to switch his mind from lamb sales to currency prices! Among the many transactions needing his attention was one to buy £3 million in euros before the weekend, and as he studied the trends he decided that as the euro had been falling against the pound while he had been away it would fall more.

But it was the pound that fell over the next few days, which cost the bank dear and woke Trev out of his holiday dreams.

The autumn seemed to go quickly. He and Naomi managed two weekends away. The one to Paris lived up to its reputation, but the second to Warsaw was anything but romantic. They actually had two extra days to add to their weekend and for the first two days Naomi found it interesting to see how the City had been rebuilt after the ravages of the last war.

Trev enjoyed it but when he had been with Jim and Marion they had talked about the threat facing English farmers from the labour intensive, barely subsistent Polish system. The figures stuck with him that in the UK just 2% of the population worked on the land whereas in Poland it was nearer 30%. Now he was in Poland he wanted to hire a car and drive out into the countryside to see just what it was like.

But Naomi was a city girl - she might enjoy nice scenery in passing but she had no interest in the people inside it. Even so the day was going reasonably well until Trev saw an elderly couple driving five cows down the lane. When they turned into a farmyard he stopped the car to have a word with them. Naomi was not too pleased.

The farming couple knew a few words of English and with the limited words that Trev had picked up from his phrase book they tried to communicate. Standing between two ramshackled wooden buildings they told him that this farm was their only living but their children worked elsewhere. There were only five cows and two heifers and two calves tethered under fruit trees in the orchard. Trev could see new saw marks on those as though the fruit trees were being pruned and next to them were several rows of soft fruit bushes. From the gestures and broken English they appeared to be an important part of the farm.

By this time Naomi had left the car and was stamping around impatiently. Reluctantly, Trev drove towards the nearest town to look round the ruins and the town centre but on the journey he noticed numerous small farms very similar to one he had looked at.

The following weekend Naomi let herself into Trev's flat early and by the time he returned there was food sizzling in the oven, candles flickering and a bottle of red wine breathing itself towards perfection. The romance continued in its old pattern, and Naomi decided to take Christmas with her sister and her family in Cambridge. He had hoped they could spend a couple of days together but Naomi was determined about her decision.

Trev wanted a bit more out of Christmas than the odd text saying 'I luv u'. He had no intention of spending Christmas day with his father; much as he loved him he just couldn't get on with his stepmother. Little older than Trev she seemed to resent his presence as though he was trying to take his Dad away from her. He could put up with the tension long enough to share an evening but nothing longer.

His own mother and stepfather always made him very welcome but the problem there was that Bob, as village butcher, worked flat out all hours in the run up to Christmas and only managed to stay awake enough to eat Christmas dinner. Afterwards he would just snore away the day in his armchair. By Boxing Day, he would be sociable enough -when awake. There were plenty of other villagers in the local to make Trev feel festive but he still could not get excited about the prospect.

Then, before he had sorted out what to do, he received a Christmas card saying. "We are on our own this Christmas so if you wish to come walking this way, why not come and stay? Love Marion and Jim."

So on the Saturday before Christmas Trev turned off the M1 towards Ashbourne, drove through Leek in the direction of

Macclesfield and a few miles out took a right up the Buxton Road at Bosley traffic lights.

On a sudden impulse and with time in hand, he drove past the bottom of the valley and on up to the ice cream farm and bought a large rum and raisin before walking outside to the benches overlooking the clough. The weather was cold and dry with a biting east wind that soon put a tingle into the ears and toes, but the air was fresh, the ice cream tasted even better than he remembered and he felt a strange sense of coming home.

Following the grey gritstone walls up to Gorsybank, Trev, having met just one Landrover, became aware of the serenity in a country community in winter. He drove past many cottages and isolated farms, some with festive lights, all showing obvious signs of occupation, but with not a person in sight. He stepped out of the car in the farmyard and was struck by the still quietness. Gone was the racket of London, the motorway hum, even the drone of his own car was now no more than a memory. Marion met him with her usual warmth. "Have you had dinner? Would you like a cup of tea? Jim's walking the moor with the dogs."

In the farmhouse kitchen the heat from the ever-burning Rayburn gave an added tranquillity. The decorations were not overdone; although there was a couple of dangling baubles hanging round the wall clock, for the rest Marion had relied on the traditional holly and ivy. As he stepped past the open lounge door Trev could hear the reassuring tick of the grandfather clock from within.

Suddenly he was back in his Grandad's home remembering his childish fascination with an old clock that had ticked away the time and the moon phases over generations. Alas it had been sold along with almost all his Grandad's possessions. With the startling suddenness of flashbacks he realised that it had been then when his parents started to bicker, his Mum had wanted that grandfather clock but his Dad had been adamant there wasn't room in their London flat. Dad had expected a legacy but Grandad had been a tenant farmer who had let both his machinery and livestock grow old with him, with the result that once his affairs had been settled there was little left over. His Mum and Dad then argued their way into a suburban home but the bickering continued through the years. It wasn't until he had left for university that they finally ended the agony with a divorce.

His memories were interrupted when Marion brought a pot of tea and three beakers to the table. The inevitable fruitcake came next but this time with a difference in that Marion called it a white Christmas cake. There was no icing but it was decorated with whole almonds and cherries across the top, and the touch of ginger in the mixed white fruits inside gave it an unusual and delicious tang. He was on his second piece when Jim walked in. "Aye you're here then lad, good."

Jim walked across to hang his tweed hat on the plate rack above the Rayburn. There was no great fuss, no bounteous evening dinner, just grilled cheese on toast with a slice or two of pear mixed in. Then afterwards a relaxing evening in the lounge lazing around a log fire with the tall grandfather clock ticking through Trev's memories.

It was nearing 9.00 on Christmas Eve with carols ringing forth from the TV, the single malt glass was nearly empty in Trev's sleepy hand and Jim had nodded off in the other armchair. Then the doorbell rang. "Trev can you see who it is, I'm just mixing the stuffing for tomorrow."

Unlocking the door he found a young couple looking at him. The girl, after a few seconds of puzzlement, answered his "Hello?" with a "And who are you, then?"

Before he could answer she was past him and walking through to the lounge. Although neither Jim nor Marion had ever mentioned her Trev now recognised her from two or three photos he had seen around the house. He had presumed that she had either died or become estranged in some way and that his friends would explain some day. The man stepping through the door next was darker skinned than Naomi but his uncared for look and straggly dreadlocks contrasted dramatically with her sophisticated elegance.

Taking a look outside he saw there was no one else coming, just a battered old Ford Escort steaming in the cold night air. He listened to the sounds from the lounge of happy reunions and he was undecided for a second as what would be most rude, to intrude or to go straight to bed. In the end he intruded and Jim introduced him to his daughter Rebecca. "We used to call her Becky now we call her Reb because she's always off at some demonstration or other."

Trev did not discover what sort of demonstrations and his

attempts at conversation with Dylan got little response than "Yeah man." Trying to think of something to say he asked, "Dylan, now that's an unusual name." "Yeah sure is, my Dad wanted a poet." Trev retired to bed early feeling a little disappointed at the unexpected turn up - and then kicking himself for being so silly. Perhaps he was just missing Naomi? Something certainly seemed to be missing.

He woke early and exchanged a couple of affectionate text messages with Naomi while dressing. Outside Christmas morning was invitingly dry and crisp, and he couldn't resist taking a walk before breakfast. Seeing Jim already out with his dogs Trev joined him for a potter round the farmyard.

Jim pointed over a loose box door at a tup. "He should be up on the moor working but some stupid hikers' have smashed some bottles up there and one piece had pushed up between his hoofs. My best tup's out of action in the breeding season, and the one I've bought to replace him just isn't in his league."

Trev sympathised, and admired the tup's long muscular body as he watched Jim deftly tip the large beast over to sit it up against his knees. Showing Trev the deep wound, Jim dressed it and saw the tup comfortable before the two men returned to the warm kitchen for breakfast.

Trev was enjoying a dish of steaming hot porridge with Jim when Rebecca came in and sat opposite him. She had a well-structured face that was spoiled by a certain tired out look, and with no makeup and untidy hair she was far from being well groomed, but her eyes suggested a lively personality. That there was a certain love-hate relationship between daughter and father was soon obvious by the way Jim looked with affection towards her and inquired what mischief she had been into.

"Dad do you mean, were we in Genoa? Well the answer is yes, we were. Dylan was only a few yards away from that poor man the police shot and then ran over. Dylan put up a good show until the police beat him up and broke his jaw, his arm and two ribs."

As Trev was trying to recall snippets he had read about the anti-globalisation riots, he watched the usual affection on Jim's face turn to anger. "Why?" he asked in anguish, "Why do it then?"

"Dad we'll only argue if I try to explain. Anyway I was in

Gothenburg in June and in Davos in January - and I'm proud of it."

Then turning to the silent and clearly mildly embarrassed Trev opposite her, she said, "That was the World Economic Forum's annual meeting in Switzerland if you don't know."

He did know but he thought it better to say nothing and decided it was time to go for Jim and Marion's presents he had left outside in the car boot. As he made his excuses and turned from the table, he realised that Marion was standing with a look of dismay right behind him. She took his arm and said to everyone, "Listen - its Christmas Day. Trev's here from London as our guest, so let's have no more bickering."

Rebecca asked, "And what does Trev do when he's in London, then?"

"I trade in currency," Trev said flatly.

Apparently it was the tradition of the farm to exchange presents over a mid-morning coffee by which time all the livestock had been tended, not that there was much to do on a hill sheep farm in mid-winter, but up to a few years before there had also been a few cows and the habit had stuck. Trev had brought Jim the very latest and most expensive lightweight all weather jacket that London had to offer, and for Marion, having noticed the well-used state of her kitchenware, a set of Le Creuset pans. That the presents would have set him back a good few hundred pounds was not lost on Rebecca, but she was rather thrown out by the gift of gloves - that had originally been intended for Marion. He also kept Jim's gloves back for the budding poet, for when he would eventually made his sleepy appearance.

They gave him a walking book of the Dark Peak - *Mostly Downhill* - which caused some merriment because to Trev's town legs most walks on the farm seemed to be exactly the opposite. And they gave him a novel by local author Erica James, which Marion said was set in their part of Cheshire.

Rebecca graciously apologised for having brought no present, and this caused Marion to put in, "If you rang home occasionally you might know a little bit more about what we were doing or who was here."

But it became a happy day; there was no more talk of globalisation or currency trading, just a superb dinner followed by a refreshing walk across the moor. From the way she strode up the rugged paths and through the heather, it was soon evident that Rebecca knew and enjoyed the countryside as much as her parents. Dylan mooched along behind and still didn't seem inspired to say anything very poetical.

On Boxing Day Marion made some of the left over turkey into a picnic and persuaded Rebecca to take the two young men off towards Three Shires Head, which was where a wonderful old packhorse bridge marked the meeting of the three counties of Cheshire, Derbyshire and Staffordshire. Having grown up in the area Rebecca was able to relate some of its history to her companions.

The next day Trev offered to treat them all to a pub lunch so Rebecca said, "Why not all go to the Ship Inn at Wincle. Then if Dad put us off further along the lane, we three can walk over to the Roaches; and Mum and Dad could meet us there for afternoon tea and bring us back?"

Jim said. "Aye, I fancy a ride out, what do you say, luv. Shall we drop 'em off and take a ride round, then pick 'em up again, say around four."

The walk was fascinating and the views were dramatic, at first high above a rushing upland river and then on the amazing rocky ridge that looks down onto an English 'loch' . But Dylan was not inspired and sounded less poetical as the day went on. The only real enthusiasm he showed was for a pile of loose stones, which he kicked and said, "I could have done with a pile of these in Genoa."

As they went Rebecca told them lots of snippets of the history of these remote hills. The walk was slow but very enjoyable and eventually they reached the tea rooms to join Jim and Marion around a large pot of tea and scones with jam and cream.

Chapter 4

Back in London, after a loving reunion with his sophisticated Naomi, Trev was soon immersed in the demands of work again. His success in the currency market was again rewarded by a handsome New Year bonus. Twice they managed a long weekend away but when he suggested going to the farm he had told her all about in Cheshire for the Easter break, she flatly refused. "Someone might see us", she said.

To be honest Trev was growing tired of the secrecy, and he began to talk of changing jobs so that their relationship could become more normal, but Naomi would not hear of it. He even began to wonder if this was the way Naomi liked it. In the end he responded to Marion and Jim's invitation and went alone to Gorsybank again.

"It might be Good Friday but I've got to work," said Jim with a smile. "The ewes are due on April 20th and that's just a week away. There's sure to be some that drop their lambs a few days early so I want to sort through them this weekend."

Trev hadn't realised that some weeks previously all the ewes had been scanned and marked, not only to find out which were expecting twins or singles but also as to when they were due. Jim explained, "I don't want the late lambers eating all the grass on my lambing paddocks, so we'll keep them away for a while."

"What about those who're expecting twins?"

"I sorted those out a couple of months ago and brought them on th' in-bye so I could give em a bit extra, but them carrying singles went back on th' moor for a while. Now we need to sort out the early lambers from the late ones."

Not that they had to man handle the heavy ewes, it was a matter of running them through the race with Jim at the far end deftly switching the small race gate back and too to separate the clearly marked sheep. Trev helped Marion to push the ewes forward so that they went past Jim in a continuous stream. Even so it took all day to sort and drive the separated flocks into their respective fields. "Without your help we couldn't have done both lots in one day." Marion said to him as they finished their tea.

They spent most of Saturday doing last minute repairs to the gates and pens in the lambing paddocks. On Sunday Trev went with Jim and Marion to morning service in the Clumber Church then treated them to Sunday lunch in a little café along the brook side.

Monday saw Trev and Jim on a morning walk round the now heavily pregnant ewes. Jim and Marion were going off to have midday dinner with some relatives beyond Buxton and Trev was intending to motor back to London in the afternoon. The ewes were still bleating and wandering restlessly about after being separated the day before. Jim explained how hill sheep may seem to be lonely animals spread about on the moor, but they are very aware when they can't find others they know. As he spoke one adventurous young ewe jumped up on the dividing wall and sent a short length of stones tumbling down. "Blast, I'll have to rebuild that or we'll have 'em all mixed up again. Marion will shoot me - I'll be late taking her to her sister's."

"Let me do it, I don't need to be home before tonight and you've given me some good lessons at it." Jim looked a bit hesitant but agreed reluctantly. He went on his way muttering something like, "I was trying to get out of it... I hate that Macclesfield to Buxton road at weekends... crazy motorcyclists... it's turned into a race track."

To get to a firm base Trev had to pull more of the wall down before he could rebuild it. Jim had told him a good wall builder always uses every stone he picks up, which means that it's important to judge both size and shape of each stone before picking it up. He knew he worked much slower than Jim would have, but it was very enjoyable. His tummy was rumbling more than the stones by the time he placed the last stone on top. Even so he decided to take a look round the in-lamb ewes before leaving and that was how he found the two young lambs. To Trev's inexperienced eye they looked premature, so he carried them towards the field corner pen with the ewe bleating and pushing round his legs.

It was growing dark by the time he pulled into the farm café for a baked potato then a thick slice of apple pie. Cutting across country to the A50 and on to the M1 Trev found it full of holiday traffic returning to London. Bank holidays! The journey was so slow and frustrating that Trev decided to break it and he pulled off at a service stop. It was only when he reached into the back seat for his topcoat that he remembered his mobile phone; he had not thought about it since taking his coat off to build the wall. There were several messages from Naomi, each one a little angrier. There was no way he could have felt his vibrating phone when it hung on the stone wall or rested on the back car seat.

Naomi would have been at his flat by 8.00, ready to release the frustration of an Easter without him, so why wasn't he answering? They had one of their rare telephone conversations but it ended in acrimony when Trev explained that he couldn't see him getting back before ten.

With the phone in his hand he decided to ring Jim to tell him about the two premature lambs. A strange woman's voice answered. "Hello, I'm Jessie, Marion's sister." When Trev explained who he was and why he was ringing she said. "On the way back from our place they were in an accident with a motor bike. They're both injured. I'm just collecting some things to take to the hospital for them."

"How bad are they?"

"Marion's got a broken wrist and some ribs, but Jim's still in the operating theatre. I think he has a badly broken leg but I'll find out more when I get there."

Jessie promised to ring him back when she knew more and Trev had a snack before continuing his journey. He was back at his flat before Jessie rang. "Jim is OK. His femur was badly broken but they have pinned it for him."

The significance of this accident at lambing time was obviously not lost on Trev so he asked, "What about the ewes lambing, Jessie?"

"Our son is going to Gorsybank tomorrow to look after things, but he can only really stay about a week because our own ewes start to lamb this weekend. Something like this is always a problem - hill flocks all lamb at the same time." She took Trev's silence as a question. "All the hill farms lamb now, it's so that the ewes and young lambs get out on the moor when the new spring growth comes. It means there is little chance of finding someone to look after the lambing."

After a restless night Trev was back in the office early but his mind was on the flock of ewes. In the end he went in to see his section director about taking a holiday. "I am afraid you're not due any holiday, Trevor. But I have to tell you we are looking for voluntary redundancies," was the blunt reply. When he showed some interest it was followed by an offer on not over generous terms. Trev agreed to take a day or two to think it over.

The text messages flashed back and fro between him and Naomi, and she brought her visit forward to Tuesday night. From a woman who he knew was prepared to sacrifice all on the altar of career and promotion, Trev was not surprised to hear that he was a fool for even thinking about it. But after tucking into an expensive take-away they put aside the argument and snuggled down in bed.

Trev took a couple of days and then he decided to put his terms to his boss. It seemed to him that the outcome would be perhaps a sign. They met his much more generous demands immediately. His mind was clear and he told Naomi what he had decided. "If you do we are finished," was her stark reply.

By the time Trev phoned Cheshire, Marion, though in considerable discomfort, was out of hospital and back at home. Her response to his offer was enthusiastic but even she pleaded with him not to give his job up just for them. Trev said. "I think I am doing this for myself more than for you. So don't you worry about me."

The flat was soon leased to a junior colleague desperate for central London accommodation and Trev was on his way by Sunday morning. A strange feeling of freedom and anticipation tingled up and down his spine as he tried to control the urge to push his foot down to the car floor. When he finally climbed out of his car in the Gorsybank yard, Marion greeted him with her usual welcoming smile and said. "I'd hug you if it wouldn't hurt so much."

Jim was in surprisingly good spirits when Trev visited him in hospital. Perhaps it was that he'd been out of bed for the first time and walked with a frame that had cheered him up. Perhaps it was that Trev was at the farm. Whichever, he seemed quite confident that Trevor would manage the sheep.

The enormity of what he had taken on hit Trev when he walked round the lambing field later that night. From what he could make out by the light of his torch about 30 ewes had lambed but as they were only from a few hours to just a day or two old, they were all still on the lambing paddocks. There was a chorus of bleats as mums and young ones tried to keep in touch amongst the other in-lamb ewe's. Trev suddenly felt it was a frightening responsibility he had rashly taken on.

Fortunately there seemed to be nothing wrong so he was able to go to bed and sleep peaceably. Despite her tiredness Marion was up earlier than Trevor and was able to walk around the fields with him before breakfast, but her ribs ached too much to come out again afterwards. As Trev walked across the farmyard towards the lambing fields, he was surprised to find Gyp falling in behind him, and when he paused to give him a pat, Gyp gave a more than half-hearted tail wag.

It was obvious that Trev would have to move some ewes and lambs out to reduce congestion; when he started to drive some of the ewe's and lambs he was even more surprised to find Gyp helping him. Most of the time the dog seemed to know what to do without Trev saying anything, at other times Gyp responded to a gesture or a word as though they had always worked together. The city boy discovered very quickly the incredible pleasure of working with animals and of an animal seemingly to understand him. It had been a long and tiring morning when man and dog walked home for a well-earned dinner.

Still feeling not too well, after the meal Marion decided to take an afternoon rest in bed. The telephone rang just as Trev was putting his coat on to go outside; it was Rebecca. "I've just rung Aunt Jessie to wish her a happy birthday and she has told me about Mum and Dad! How are they? Why are you there, anyway?"

"Your mother is having a rest at the moment, her ribs are painful but otherwise she seems all right; and your father's operation has been successful."

"Great, so why are you there?"

"I've come to help with the ewe's and I hope to stay till your father is fit again."

"God, what can a city boy like you do with lambing sheep, especially when they're out in the open in the sort of weather we get at home?"

Trev tried to reassure her.

"No. No, this is no good. No, I'll get the next train out. Can you meet me if I ring from the station when I get there this evening."

"That's no problem, country girl. It will be a pleasure."

They had just finished their tea when the Rebecca rang to say she was at the station. Marion had seemed both pleased and disturbed when he had told her Rebecca was coming home, now she was determined to come with Trev to the station because, as she put it, "I don't want her being difficult with you; I'll come along to keep the peace."

Trev put her battered rucksack in the boot while Marion had a painful reunion with her daughter. Rebecca apologised for the too enthusiastic a hug and the two women then chatted happily all the way back to the farm.

The next morning Trev was down and had the kettle boiling by six o'clock. "Good - make one for me." A sleepy voice said from the hall doorway.

Trev turned round to see a tussled looking Rebecca walking towards him. They munched a biscuit, slurped down the hot coffee and slipped into wellington-boots and topcoats before Rebecca even spoke again. "Now we are in this together you'd better call me Reb like everyone else."

"How do you do, Reb." he jested and put his hand out and shook hers firmly.

There were many new lambs in each of the three lambing paddocks, but the sound created as the getting to know you process took place was like music compared to London traffic. In the second paddock one ewe was struggling to lamb, and it took Trev and Gyp just a brief moment to catch it, but it took him a bit longer to ease the large lamb into the world.

I am afraid it's dead, he said sadly to Rebecca. But Reb dropped on her knees and started to pummel its chest and blow down its throat. It was a few moments before she would admit defeat and accept that it was indeed dead. Finally she looked up at the Trev and, with a determined twinkle in her eye, she said, "Well we can't win 'em all - and anyway I saw twins in the other paddock that look short of milk. You skin this while I go and catch one of them."

Trev slipped the skinning knife out of its scabbard and started work. It had looked easy when he had watched Jim do it but the slimy skin slipped through his fingers. As he hacked away with the knife, he heard Reb's little chuckle behind him.

When he finally dragged the skin off the carcass and held it up in triumph, she said, "I've seen a few skinned over the years but I've never seen one made into a string vest before."

They were both laughing so much that they had a job to push the little lamb's feet into the right holes in the skin. When they finally got the skin to cover his back the little fellow staggered off to the watching ewe. Although she claimed him as her own, there were so many pieces of tattered skin hanging down the side of him he looked as though he had ten legs.

On the way out they discovered two ewes and four lambs in an agitated muddle, One mother appeared to be claiming three of the lambs, and Trev was unsure as to who belonged to whom, but Reb could tell by their colour which belonged to each ewe. Reb carried two lambs up the field well away from the other two, and at a word from Trev, Gyp sat watchful halfway between the two ewes, which discouraged either from trying to pinch the others lambs. When things had settled down Reb said, "That will do" to Gyp. But he just ignored her and sat there until Trev gave a whistle. Stamping her foot in frustration she said to him, "I've just realised; that dog has not responded to any one of my commands." Gyp just wagged his tail and trotted behind Trev with his tongue hanging out in a cheeky way.

Marion had breakfast ready by the time they got back to the farmhouse, and it was much more enjoyable than a bacon bap. It was obvious that she was still in quite a lot of pain and wouldn't be able to help round the sheep for a while.

So Trev and Reb fell into an enjoyable working routine; lambs came thick and fast keeping them both busy from morning til night. Trev found that Reb was a knowledgeable companion and she was happy to give advice when he got into difficulty without rubbing it in - and he wasn't too proud to ask. The fact that Gyp would only work for him made him feel much better - he really felt valued as a person by the dog so choosing him.

Marion went in to see Jim most days. Sometimes neighbours or relatives would drive her there, at other times Reb drove her to the hospital. It was then that Trev found immense satisfaction from being alone in the lambing paddocks, caring for this flock of sheep who were dependent on him and his decisions. During a quiet few minutes he was resting in the hut with Gyp lying outside - not being a house dog he preferred not to come into the hut - when Reb, just back from the hospital, came in with a flask of tea. "So how does this compare to high finance in London?"

"It's great; it beats anything the city has to offer."

"You might find the difference at the end of the year, I doubt whether Dad's total profits for the year would reach £10,000. Do you think you could live on that, city boy?"

Trev sipped his tea and remained quiet, particularly as to the fact that his last year's bonus had been over a hundred times more. She took his silence as an argument and went on, "That's how I got involved in these protests, Dad's profits slumped because greedy money traders were driving up the pound against the euro, which collapsed farm prices here. *They* get fat, while small businessmen like Dad go under, lose their livelihoods and lose their hope."

When Trev turned to look at her he suddenly realised that she was taking more care about her appearance; her hair had been brushed until it had a shine, there was a clean and smart jumper beneath the heavy coat and there was a hint of lipstick. She looked vastly different to the girl who came knocking on the door last Christmas Eve with her hairy poet. "Tell me, where is the poet?" he suddenly thought aloud.

"He wouldn't know what to do in a field of sheep - and you are changing the subject - what about the difference between Dad's profits and your big bonus money, city trader?"

"Countries have been trading in currency since Roman times, there has to be some way of equalling values between different nations. And if a country's currency goes up too high, it prices itself out of the market and its currency begins to fall back again. My job was just to guess forward and try to have the right currency at the right time - for the benefit of my customer."

When Reb snorted in derision, Trev added, "Well that's just how the world works. Anyway it's all behind me now; there are just these old sheep and you until you go on your next protest march. When's your next protest?"

"There is a G-7 in Canada in early June; I intend to be there."

Trev remained quiet. In his former life he would have held on to every word coming out of such a finance meeting, now it seemed a world away and suddenly he didn't care. "Let's go and look round the sheep again, they are a lot more interesting than money."

Floss, Marion's dog, had now began to attach herself to Reb, but the dog was not very brave and seldom came into the lambing fields, choosing instead to lie outside the gate, safely away from protective mother sheep. When they stepped out of the door, not only had she come to the hut, she was now clasped in the amorous embrace of Gyp. Trev vaguely knew that bitches come on heat twice a year but he was too inexperienced to have read the signs in Marion's Floss. Now it was too late, to his sudden embarrassment, Gyp and Floss were coupled up. Reb was highly amused, "How are you going to explain that to Mum, city boy?"

Soon a week had gone by, and then another, and another. Marion was getting stronger but Jim was still in hospital, although they were talking about him coming home in about a week. The bulk of the sheep had now lambed which allowed Trev and Reb time to take an evening walk down to the valley for a drink in the local. He found her pleasant and relaxing company, as long as they stayed off the subject of world summits and multinational companies.

At the far end of the farm buildings to the farmhouse stood a semi derelict cottage, and as they walked past Reb explained that her Dad used to have a man living there until things got tighter a few years before. Now it stood empty. Trev was obviously interested so the next day Reb brought the key and invited him to go in and look round. Trev pushed the broken gate inwards and walked up the very short garden path. He admired the grey rugged stone. "Look Reb, isn't that amazing, after the generations of weathering, these lintels still show the chisel marks of the old craftsmen who made them."

The door creaked open to reveal the cobweb-draped windows. It was not large, just a kitchen, a pantry and a large living room downstairs, and two bedrooms and a bathroom upstairs. In one place the stonework had slipped but the view from the main room window across the valley was terrific, even the windows themselves with their carved stone mullions - Reb said they originated from a derelict hall demolished long ago - gave the room real character. Trev stood transfixed; in his imagination he pictured an old but familiar shepherd, smoke drifting upwards from his pipe, gazing across the valley. But he decided to keep his thoughts to himself.

Jim came home out of plaster but still on crutches. Before going into the house he walked carefully across the yard to look down the in-bye fields. In the warmth of the afternoon sun young lambs scampered playfully round their mothers. "They look a grand lot; you've done very well lad, I'm grateful."

Jim was home; Marion's ribs no longer hurt; and now when they were out in the fields, Reb and Trev had begun to laugh together companionably. Then Reb received a phone call. The next day she told her mother that she was taking a train for London that afternoon. 'Why do you have to go now; we're all just getting straight, Reb." protested Marion. But she had her reply ready, "You're both going to be all right now and that city man might just make a shepherd if you keep an eye on him."

Marion drove her to the station that afternoon. The farm seemed quiet without her. The conversation seemed strained over tea and sensing that the other two would like to be alone Trev decided to take a walk outside. The warm evening drew him to the stone seat that looked over the in-bye fields. The setting sun still peeped over the western hills on the other side of the valley. He pondered why she had gone and just what she thought she could change? As the sun slipped out of sight its rays radiated across the sky touching scattered clouds with gold and orange. Although she had gone, her laughter and teasing banter lingered in his mind, and he felt happy.

Gradually as the sun sank, shadows obscured the hillside, trees and stone walls blurred until just the outer edge of the hill was highlighted. Ewes called for their lambs, a passing peewit called overhead and the hoot of an owl was heard in the distance.

Perhaps coming straight from one relationship had left him vulnerable, he thought. Not that there had been any romance between him and Reb, and yet somehow there had been something intangible but very strong developing between them over the last few weeks.

Chapter 5

Trev had one disappointment after Jim's return; Gyp would no longer follow him. When Jim came out Gyp followed him like a shadow, and when he went into the house Gyp lay waiting by the door. Much to everyone's amusement he even crept inside the house to curl up by Jim's feet.

Trev missed the dog's company nearly as much as he missed his help, and he needed his help because last year's ewe lambs, called shearlings, which had wintered on a low land farm and returned to the moor in March, now needed to be brought off again. Gem would do the outrun but she wasn't good at pushing the sheep when they gathered into one large flock. Although Gem responded well to his commands he had learnt not to trust her, once the sheep were penned Gem would sneak away to go on a parish tour and there was nothing sheep farmers hated more than a rambling dog. More than once Trev had done his own parish tour trying to find her. It wasn't such a problem out on the hill though; Gem never left a roundup.

But it was in the latter stages that the more forceful Gyp was needed. Jim obviously couldn't go striding across the moor so in the end Trev took Gyp on a lead and held him until Gem, and Floss, who was working for Marion on the other flank, had worked the sheep into one large straggly flock. Fortunately Gyp now decided to work for him and they managed to make the gather. Once the sheep were off the moor Gyp soon ran back to his master again, but Floss and Gem could handle them from there on.

Jim was making such a quick recovery the physiotherapists soon replaced his crutches with two metal walking sticks. The farmer hated these and cut two of his more battered shepherd's crooks down to the right length. "Nothing can beat the feel of horn." he claimed stubbornly.

Trev had been thinking about the cottage. Marion had explained that the landlord wanted to sell it but as Jim had a lifetime tenancy of both the farm and the cottage they couldn't sell it without his agreement. When he and Jim were walking across the field together he decided to be bold and grasp the bull by the horns. "Are you going to let the landlord sell the cottage, Jim?"

Jim stopped and leaned on his two shepherds crooks, "Only if they'll pay me a handsome lump sum to give up the tenancy. Anyway I'm not sure that I want some yuppie living right by my farmyard, complaining about the noise and the smell."

"How about me?" Trev jumped in. "Could you put up with me living right by the farmyard?"

"Now let's get one thing straight lad; you've been a big help and I'm going to pay you for the work you've done, but there is no way I can afford to take a man on full time."

"I don't want paying, Jim. For me it's been a complete break - and an education; I just want to extend it. If I can persuade the estate to sell the cottage to me, could you and I agree a price for you to give up the tenancy? It would include me working with you for a year - not for you mind - but with you. After that... well we will have to see."

Swinging his crooks instep again Jim walked on across the field. "I'll have to talk to Marion about it; but I think we could come to an agreement. But can you afford it, Trev?"

Trev just nodded. He thought it better not to mention his city bonus had been for the last four years and that after paying tax all of it was in a good bank, just waiting. Yes he could afford it.

Although the estate's agent was keen to be rid of a semi-derelict cottage he pretended otherwise and set a high price. Trev was not so easily caught and set about bartering him down; it took a few weeks of argument before they settled, but finally they did. Trev agreed to Jim's price for the tenancy without an arguement.

Floss duly produced three pups, two bitches and one dog. "You'd better choose yourself a pup," Jim said, "but not the dog. Two dogs on one farm will end up fighting." he said, with a twinkle in his eye. Trev couldn't resist one of the little females, nearly all black with just a narrow white collar, a white belly and a pretty white spot round one eye.

As for the cottage Trev could see no need to make any major alterations but it could stand some 'poshing up'. Part of one bulging wall needed rebuilding, and as it was the end wall in the lounge he decided to leave the new stonework exposed and have the rest of the living room re plastered. The beams that were already exposed would stand a clean up. Jim knew the local craftsmen well - in fact as was the way in the countryside, most were either related to him in one way or another or had gone to school with him.

It wasn't long before they were at work in the cottage. One-bedroom needed very little doing to it so Trev decorated it himself and bought the furniture including an impressive king-sized bed. But he could not move in quite yet until the kitchen was modernised to his satisfaction.

There had been a few text messages from Naomi saying she missed him - wasn't he bored with the countryside yet? Then he received one telling him that there was a vacancy in a money trading section, would he like to apply? Trev decided he should give her a ring and explain about the cottage and his deal with Jim for the year. Naomi couldn't believe him and invited herself down for that weekend. When he told Marion she suggested that she could sleep in Reb's bedroom and he decided not to explain their relationship back in London.

Naomi looked fabulous as she walked down the platform towards him. Even an extra hour on the train journey, due to a delay, had failed to ruffle her elegance and sophistication. Her greeting was warm and her enthusiasm to see where he was living was engaging. On the journey back to the farm the rain set in, Naomi wasn't used to the kind of weather that hits the Pennines with such a vindictive vengeance. They stopped off at the cottage first; laughing as they ran in doors out of the heavy rain and with bewildering speed they were soon upstairs trying out the new bed. It was some time before Trev took her over to the farmhouse to introduce her to the others.

The following morning it was still raining when Trev went outside to check round and give the dogs a run. When he returned to the farmhouse for breakfast he found Marion and Naomi gossiping away like old friends and they all had a very enjoyable breakfast together. Naomi said, "Trev. Can I join you when you walk round the mummy sheep and baby lambs this morning?"

Trev looked out of the window. "The rain seems to have stopped. Why not - but I warn you, it will be muddy."

"That's alright, I've been shopping. You wait till you see my super new lightweight jacket, and I've bought some guaranteed waterproof suede boots."

Where the ewes had trampled round the gateways the soil had turned to greasy mud and even out on the pastures the going was awful.

Naomi's new suede boots were soon coated and the mud began to work up the sides of her jeans as she slipped trying to keep up with Trev.

"B---- me, Trev, how can you enjoy this?"

Trev walked to a young lamb. Naomi thought it was asleep, but when Trev picked up the lifeless form by its hind legs he said. "A cold night's rain'll test any weakly lamb. This one's a twin and the mother has wandered off with the other twin.

When, further on, he picked up another dead lamb, Naomi said, "How can you take it so casually. These poor lambs have died of cold and all you say is 'ah well you always lose some'.

He tried to explain but when they got back to the farm and opened a loose box where he had been treating an old ewe with mastitis. The vet had left antibiotics but she lay there dead. "The poor little lambs," Naomi said, almost sobbing. "How can you be so heartless?" .

When Marion saw the state of Naomi's posh boots and jeans she bustled her into the house and upstairs for a bath and change of clothing. Jim chuckled as he watched Trev turn the hosepipe on the suede boots before putting them by the cooker to dry. It took an hour for Naomi to reappear and when she did she looked her usual elegant self again.

Trev had promised her a bar lunch at the pub in the valley, and when they got there her spirits soon lifted. It was the first real country pub she had seen. Stone flagged floor, genuine rustic beams, and stuffed animals on ledges and in windows set the scene. Some of Jim's neighbours, who had called in for a Saturday lunchtime pint, greeted Trev with their soft hill farmer accents. Naomi was amused but it was really in a superior way, and she was soon pointing out that the food lacked London's class.

Then Trev took her for a ride along the valley through Wincle and on through the market town of Leek towards the beautiful Derbyshire dales. Through country lanes they came to Ilam and the Dove Valley. They stopped at Tissington and strolled the length of the village. They looked through the church and enjoyed an afternoon tea in the old Smithy tearooms.

Back at the farmhouse Marion and Jim had delayed their tea in anticipation of Trev and Naomi joining them. As was the custom they had had their main meal at midday and Marion had prepared a salad tea;. But it wasn't really to Naomi's taste and she picked at it. The conversation seemed to be going along well enough until Jim said, "Trev, the kennel man's been and collected the dead ewe and lambs. It seemed to put the town girl completely off her food.

After tea and back in the cottage they managed another visit to the new bed, but afterwards Naomi looked bored. "What can we do now? What about going to local wine bar. Perhaps you can show me the local lights?"

"A wine bar?" Trev puzzled. "I don't think I've really been out of the village in the evening since I came here. I suppose they might have wine bars in Macclesfield?" In the end she settled for a drink in the local, but the people were mostly Saturday night diners who had motored out to enjoy a meal in a rural surrounding, all in their individual private groups. It left the two of them alone at the bar. When Naomi complained it lacked atmosphere they walked back up to the cottage where, in the fading evening light they tried out the bed once more. Naomi said, "It's no wonder country people have big families - there's nothing else to do in this godforsaken place."

On Sunday morning Naomi decided not to walk the fields again with Trev; instead she said she would take the midday train back to London. Without a word said, there seemed to be a finality about their goodbye kiss on the station platform.

The week was going to be a busy one for it was time to put the ewes and lambs out on the moor. Fortunately the in-bye fields were well fenced so the ewes were in three separate flocks, which made it easy to deal with one flock each day. Trev got the pens ready while Jim walked slowly out into the field with his dogs. As the sheep gathered into a tighter flock by the sorting pens there was a pandemonium of noise and movement as small lambs got separated from their mothers and each called for the other. The lambs had to be marked, castrated and docked today; the latter two achieved by placing a strong rubber band on the tup lamb's pouch and on all the lamb's tails which cut off blood supply. After a few initial kicks it did both tasks painlessly.

The marking was a little more complex. Jim explained,"You see, each farm has its own flock mark, handed down through generations. We take a little nick, in exactly the same spot, out of each of our lamb's right ear." Armed with the little special nippers and the castrating implement, Jim could put the rings on and nip the ear almost as quickly as Trev and Marion could catch the lambs and bring them to him. As each was done they were lifted over the fence into the next pen. The noise was deafening as mums and babies called to each other, and when it was done they let them out onto the drive leading up to the moor where each lamb and mother were soon reunited.

It had been a long and tiring morning and Trev was pleased yet again to find that one of Marion's beef stews had been simmering away in the oven. After, Trev went up to his room and fell fast asleep on the bed - it was nearly two hours later when he woke. He dashed outside to find that Jim had started to drive the ewes and lambs towards the moor. It was a quick trot up the hill to catch him up. "Sorry about that Jim. I seemed to have dropped off into a really deep sleep." Jim said with a knowing grin, "Perhaps you have had a tiring weekend."

Even though some of the ewes had taken the lambs on to the moor on their own it took most of the afternoon to get the rest there and check that all of them had got reunited. Trev felt the deep satisfaction of watching the ewes and lambs fanning out across the fresh green heather. The moor was lovely; there were white heads of cotton grass bobbing in the breeze, curlews were calling in the distance and the peewits were swooping in noisy protest when a ewe got too close to their chicks. And the inevitable carrion crow flapped his undertaker's wings in hopeful anticipation that there might be at least one casualty.

The next day they had it to do all over again, with the ewes and lambs from the second field, and on the third day the final part of the flock was tackled. There were still about 50 ewes left in the lambing paddocks - the last to lamb. In fact there were still three stragglers left to lamb. At the end of the day Trev was almost too tired to sleep and when sleep did come he was catching lambs all night. Although his tired limbs helped him forget his weekend with Naomi, he felt a terrible restlessness; it had reminded him what he had been missing.

"Have you heard from Reb, yet?" he asked Marion. "She's phoned to say she's all right - but she didn't seem to want to talk about Canada - but then she probably knows I don't really want to hear about that." He could hear the sadness in her voice as she spoke of her daughter.

Chapter 6

By mid-July Trev had moved into his own house. Although it was far from finished he managed with just the kitchen and bedroom which were now transformed. Little Spot, old enough to leave her mother for a few hours each evening, pottered about with him like a little shadow. He tried a couple of text messages to Naomi without reply, but the third got a very firm response he half expected - "Goodbye Trev. He felt a great emptiness but fondling little Spot's ears helped a little.

It was soon time to shear, and to worm dose the ewes and lambs. Just as all the sheep had a nick in the same place in one ear, they also had a raddle - or paint - mark on one shoulder. Now, of course, each ewe had to have that mark replaced after shearing.

They gathered the flock in the cool of Tuesday morning and penned them overnight in one of the lambing paddocks. The next morning a team of New Zealand contractors, who came over for the shearing season, came early and did the job in one mad hectic day. Trev's task was to put the raddle mark on each ewe after it was sheared, while Jim, still limping a little, kept the ewes flowing into the catching pens.

And it really was a hectic day; the few times Trev had a moment to spare, he watched in amusement as the shorn sheep ran into the field, where the young lambs, answering their mothers call, were faced with a strange white animal and were afraid to approach it. Eventually they overcame their fear to suckle contentedly again. The evening was well gone by the time he collapsed wearily into his own kitchen chair.

The whole flock was kept in the lambing fields overnight. On the following morning they were penned again so that the lambs could be given a worming drench and marked.

The in-bye fields, which had had no livestock on them since the ewes and lambs went on to the moor, were now ready to be cut for hay. As soon as Jim saw the weather set fair for three or four days, his old tractor and mower came out of the shed, and after a bit of training Trev was soon turned loose with it. With sunshine and a warm breeze the weather was ideal and after letting the grass lie for a day, and then shaking it up for two days with an ancient tedder, it had soon changed to lovely hay. A contractor came on the fourth day with a pick-up-baler to complete the task. Then it took Jim and Trev, with some help from Marion, three more days to cart all those bales into the Dutch barn.

After tea that night, and with little Spot trotting behind, he walked round to the Dutch barn, just to stand and admire his first harvest. Jim's voice came from behind him, "It's a great thing lad to see your harvest in the shed. Eh, an' it's been a lot easier with your help."

They both stood in silent companionship just admiring the stack of fresh green hay in the open sided barn. The smell was terrific; nicer than any bunch of flowers. Jim said, "You know, rye grass, when it's made in sunshine, is the sweetest smelling hay there is. Eh and seeing it's all in - and if you're agreeable - Marion and me thought we might have a few days away; what do you think?"

Trev knew that they had not had a holiday for a few years and he also knew that the next big task was not until mid-September when they had to gather the sheep in again to wean the tup lambs - or wether lambs as Jim insisted he called them.

"Yes, of course you can. Why don't you take a few weeks, you both need a good break - sorry, I didn't mean that as a joke." Trev replied, as Jim doubled up in laughter. And he thought he had never seen Jim look so happy since he had known him. It seemed as if he had had a great weight taken from him.

And so Trev found himself on his own in charge of a farm. Not that there was a lot to do, it was mainly a matter of walking the moor each day and checking walls and fences. Gyp became his faithful companion again and even Floss began to follow him. Spot was still too young to go out on a half-day walk but she loved to potter around the yard with him, and as for Gem - all she wanted to do was to round up sheep or visit the neighbours, so he still had to keep a wary eye on her when she was loose or shut her up.

Marion had insisted that he slept at the farmhouse while they were away. He often had to answer the phone, either to take a business call or to answer relative's questions, so when the phone rang on the third night he was surprised when it was Reb. She was at Macclesfield station and expecting her Mum to pick her up. Trev immediately offered his services.

It was a very subdued Reb who rode quietly home with him and even when he brewed a pot of tea and cut her a chunk of one of Marion's carrot cakes she said little more than thank you. Over breakfast the next morning she was still very quiet for Reb - but to Trev's surprise she asked if she could walk the moor with him. Trev carried a rucksack containing hand shears and a bottle of sheep dip in case he saw a sheep flyblown. Not that there were many but if there was one it was much easier to catch it there and then than have to come back and try to find it later. With Gyp's help it usually took only a few minutes to catch, clip out the dirty wool and wash out the maggots with the dip.

To walk the whole moor was a very long morning so he usually included a flask of tea and a chunk of the cake Marion had left for him. He had only needed to treat one sheep since Jim left but it was just his luck to see one when Reb was out with him. Turning to bite at its own wool where it was dirty near its tail the young lamb was in obvious discomfort. Gyp and Trev cornered both ewe and lamb by some rocks while Reb crept in and caught the lamb. He clipped the wool off its bottom and rubbed the dip in with a rubber glove to displace the maggots. "That's one farm smell I just can't get used to." he complained to Reb, "You know even with my glove off the smell seems to cling to my hand."

They were close to the rock where he had sat all those months before, when under Jim's supervision he had helped his first lamb into the world. "Shall we have a break," Trev suggested. He told her the story of his first day as a 'sheep farmer' and they laughed at other shared experiences while she poured the tea out and unwrapped the cake. "I am sure this cake smells of sheep dip," he said in disgust. She grabbed his piece of cake and threw it away in mock disgust. They had a good laugh again, but suddenly Reb said, "I've come home to stay, if Mum and Dad will have me. I'm going to get a job."

Trev looked at her for a few moments, "What about the protests?"

"I think I have had enough of it. Enough of the violence, enough of the life I've been leading... and I suppose of the people I've been sharing it with." She spoke slowly and then sat silently with her thoughts. Trev didn't know what to say, but she broke the silence. "Oh I'm being thoughtless, aren't I; with you in the house is there room for me now?" Trev decided not to answer. "It's time we headed back," he said.

Back in the farmyard he knew he had two or three meals in his freezer in the cottage and of course he had a microwave, so as Reb was going towards the farmhouse, he said, "Why don't you have dinner with me?"

Reb had no idea what he was talking about so he took hold of her hand and led her towards his cottage. She knew nothing of him buying the cottage. "Gosh this has changed," she gasped as they entered the kitchen. The decorators had finished in the main room and it stood empty waiting for him to buy the furniture, and with the broken glass in the back window replaced he had another splendid view across the pasture field where it rose steeply up to the moor. Reb wandered on through the house while Trev heated up two dinners and laid the table.

"You've gone to town here. Has Dad let you take over the tenancy of this place then?" she asked.

"It's all done and dusted. I've bought it," he explained.

They sat down side by side on his kitchen chairs and tucked into the Marks and Sparks specials. Reb was busy catching up on all the local gossip and Trev was happy to fill her. "I wonder how Mum and Dad are managing in Scotland." she asked. "I'm glad you have let them get away, they really needed a change.

"Are you going to show me what else you've been doing in the cottage then. Have you bought the furniture for the lounge yet?" She asked as they walked through.

When he explained that he planned to go and choose furniture later in the week, she said, "Oh good, can I come and help you choose it?" The next half hour was spent discussing ideas for the room. She liked the room, and he liked her ideas.

Later they walked down to the farmyard where he introduced her to little Spot. And then Trev decided to move his things out of the farm house. "You don't need to do this," Reb protested.

"I don't think your parents would approve of us two sleeping un-chaperoned in their house together," he said

"They are not here and anyway I don't want to be alone, please stay."

He carried on regardless, pouring oil on the argument by inviting her to go down to the pub with him later for a meal and a drink.

Later on, and to his surprise, Reb arrived at the cottage looking smartly dressed in new jeans and jumper, and of course a waterproof coat just in case. The local was warm and welcoming and although they didn't take a credit card, Trev used his cheque book to good effect on the best meal he had enjoyed for some time.

Neither had consumed too much wine but they were both feeling very companionable on the walk home. When they came to parting outside Trev's cottage, Reb said, "I don't want to go back to the farmhouse on my own. I'm not used to an empty house on my own."

Trev put a comforting arm round her shoulders, which suddenly became a full embrace ending in a long kiss. "I need your company tonight." she said. "I came back hoping you would still be here, you know."

It was all moving too quick. Trev was thinking fast. Having just come out of one amorous relationship which, with hindsight, he thought, had been far from satisfactory, if he was now to start something with Reb, it had to have more to it than just what took place in the bedroom. Perhaps Reb sensed his hesitation. She pulled back, "Are we moving too fast. Perhaps we ought to take it more slowly and get to know each other more."

"That's how I feel, I think Reb. We're both just out of another relationship and my head tells me that we should take our time. But I'm not sure that I can act that sensibly."

They held each other for a while in silence, and then Reb said. "I still don't want to sleep in that big farmhouse on my own tonight, can your head keep you under control?"

"I think so - if you don't tempt me too much."

They both laughed and held hands as they walked towards the farmhouse.

Chapter 7

It rained heavily overnight and was still raining the next morning when Trev let the dogs loose for a run. He was only going about 200 yards before returning to feed and shut them up again, but on the way back when he saw a gate open into the sorting pens and dipping area. He had been cleaning them earlier with a local dairy farmer and his tractor and vacuum tank, to suck out the used sheep dip. Perhaps he hadn't fastened the gate. Jim was paranoid about keeping sheep out of there; only the year before a stray dog had chased some lambs into the pens and nine were drowned.

Trev didn't stop to think, he just strode across the corner of the field and reached for the gate. It was a mistake. The muddy wet ground sloped upwards to the gate and as he reached out for the gate his feet shot sideways and his hand missed the gate - but his head didn't.

Trev hadn't bothered to zip up his fancy new waterproof, he had just closed a press-stud on the wind flap. He woke up to discover that he was lying on his back with his coat wide open, the rain soaking into his clothes; and when he rolled groggily onto his knees he slipped again and found himself lying on his face with the mixed smell of rotting sheep dung and sheep dip all too close to him. This was certainly something city life had not prepared him for.

By the time he had swilled most of it off with the hose pipe he was wet from head to toe. But now as he called the dogs to shut them up before going for a shower he discovered Gem was missing. He stripped off by the washing machine in the large farm house back kitchen and left a pile of clothes and a trail of footsteps across the floor as he headed towards the stairs in his pants. He met Reb sitting dejectedly halfway down the stairs. "Hello city boy, your not going to get fresh this early in the morning are you?"

"Not until I've had a shower anyway." he said, stepping past her.

"Wow, if that is some sort of new manly after-shave you're wearing I should tell you it's not going to work."

Shower gel, plenty of aftershave and clean clothes still didn't mask the sheep pen odour. In the kitchen Reb had laid the table for a cold breakfast and brewed a pot of tea, but she seemed strangely subdued as

Trev hurried his food before going to look for Gem.

Knowing which of Jim's neighbours the dog usually headed for Trev strode out briskly in that direction and Reb caught up with him as he crossed the yard. Trev's walking had improved dramatically; there was no longer that city shuffle. Now each stride reached forward with bent knee powering him across the muddy uneven ground. Reb was unable to match his strides but fortunately as they reached the first field boundary they saw Gem coming towards them across the field. "It helps a dog to return home if she hasn't been fed." Trev laughed.

"A good job, because I couldn't have gone any further at that pace."

When Trev turned he realised it was the first time that morning he had looked at her properly and he saw red-rimmed eyes blinking from a tear stained face. "Gosh you look terrible, are you ill or something?"

Bursting into tears Reb leaned on the wall with her face buried in her arms. He put a comforting arm round her shoulders and felt her shaking with sobs. "What's the matter?"

"I thought I would be all right now, but this morning I feel terrible. It's a long story really. I was so unhappy on the Canada trip."

"How do you mean?"

"I'd enjoyed it so much.... being at home here through the lambing. I can't explain it, but on the flight out to Canada it all suddenly seemed pointless; I mean the demonstrating. I suddenly felt it wasn't going to change anything, to improve anyone's life. All I seemed to be doing was ruining my own life."

"Why didn't you come straight back home?"

"I couldn't; you see it's all organised. They only pay for my flight ticket back after the demonstration. We had a couple of weeks to wait and I was so miserable. And then taking cannabis - they all do - it only made me worse."

"What about Dylan."

"There's nothing between us now. It's all over."

"So why do you feel so bad this morning?"

"My return plane ticket was an open one so I decided to take off into the countryside there for a few days. I just wanted to be on my own... to have time to think. I got talking to a man who was driving a load of horses across country - he seemed okay so I went with him."

"You were taking a bit of a risk."

"No, he was old enough to be my father - I knew he was alright.

"Because of the long distances over there they have special farms where horses can be unloaded, a sort of horse motel where they do what they call 'bale and breakfast'. It's just hay and rest for the horses, and bed and breakfast for the driver. There's even a bunkhouse with a separate room for women.

Unfortunately I went down with some sort of a virus and I had to stay there while he went on. The couple on the farm were very nice and looked out for me but it was about a fortnight before I felt up to travelling again. It was interesting; you know, horses came and went nearly every night. When I did feel a bit better they arranged for me to travel to the airport with another load of horses."

"It still doesn't explain why you feel so ill this morning?"

"That virus seemed to hang on, and the journey took it out of me again, so when I got back to London I stayed with a friend. I needed to be sure what I really wanted, I suppose. I don't know.... I seemed confused. I saw a doctor in London who gave me some tablets to help."

"But I know now what I want is here... and I've come home to start again. But this morning it all seemed wrong again. I suppose I'm a bit frightened," she said trying to wipe the tears from her eyes. Trev pulled out his handkerchief out and offered it to her. "The doctor said to take it easy for a few weeks, and not to drink with the tablets. I suppose yesterday I walked a long way with you.... and then we shared that bottle of wine.... now I feel terrible."

Later with Gem shut up again and Reb upstairs in bed, Trev set out for a walk - and to do some thinking. The thought of Reb and her protests, and her taking drugs was worrying him. Before he realised it he was out on the moor, and apart from the occasional bleat of sheep, it was quiet. Now the summer breeding season was over he missed the curlews and plovers. He had watched them flocking together a few weeks ago and knew that by now they would be wading in the shallows of an estuary somewhere.

He walked on aimlessly, alone with his thoughts and the sheep, when suddenly a covey of grouse burst in to wing just in front of him and startled him back to reality. He watched them skimming the heather in a tight formation before dipping down beyond a small rise in the ground. Their gravelly calls told him that they had landed and would now be running through the heather. He looked at the heather, it had been in flower for a while and was now over its best but its vivid purple was still startling, and he couldn't believe he had walked so far without marvelling at its beauty again.

By the time he returned he had sorted his mind. Perhaps thinking about Jim, and even more Marion, had helped him decide. He knew where she came from. Yes, he had no doubt that this unusual but very attractive country girl was going to play a big part in his life.

He hadn't realised that it was mid-afternoon until he opened the kitchen door and the appetising smell of frying bacon hit his nostrils - and his stomach. Reb turned from the cooker to greet him. "I've had a good sleep and feel much better now. And I'm as hungry as a horse; how about you?"

"It smells great, put three more rashers in while I wash my hands."

Trev had not realised just how hungry he was until he sat down to that plate of egg and bacon. Reb kept apologising for her behaviour earlier - and for the past few years of her life.

But by the next morning she was back to her usual energetic self. While Trev went about the business on the farm, Reb was searching the situations vacant columns. In the afternoon they visited Arighi Bianchi in Macclesfield - the best furniture store for many miles around. Trev soon discovered that Reb had a much better eye for colours than him, but it was surprising just how much they had in common. By the end of a long and tiring afternoon they had ordered the complete lounge furnishings from carpet to curtains.

Two weeks later the holiday-makers returned. "I couldn't believe it Reb when you answered the phone the other night," Marion said with a smile. "It's great to have you home again." And as Reb gave Jim a dutiful kiss, he joked, "When are you off again?"

Marion now sensed Reb's embarrassed silence. "What have you two been up to..... You've got something to tell us, haven't you?"

"You're right, Mum. I'm back for good!" Then Reb took hold of Trev's hand. "You tell them."

It's a long story," said Trev. "Perhaps you should come and see our new furniture..... we are in the cottage together now.